any boy but you

a
North Pole, Minnesota
novel

any boy but you

a
North Pole, Minnesota
novel

JULIE HAMMERLE

Entangled Publishing, LLC
2614 South Timberline Road
Suite 109
Fort Collins, CO 80525
Visit our website at www.entangledpublishing.com.

Crush is an imprint of Entangled Publishing, LLC.

Edited by Kate Brauning
Cover design by Erin Dameron-Hill
Cover art from iStock

Manufactured in the United States of America

First Edition February 2017

For John

Chapter One

"Prince's skates are half-off, you know."

"Good for Prince's," Elena Chestnut said, counting to ten in her head as she struggled to conceal her annoyance. There was only one customer in Chestnut's Sporting Goods—Craig, North Pole's own...What? Goofball? Court jester? Pain in the butt? He'd been in the store for half an hour, quizzing Elena on prices and wondering about future sales. He'd already asked about the tennis rackets, skis, and ladies' golf gloves. Now he was on ice skates.

"It's just, you know, the end of the season." Craig frowned. "Maybe you should think about offering a deal on skates."

Elena's irritation bubbled again. Craig was not merely the only customer in the store right now, he was the only customer she'd seen all day. *Just* buy *something already*. She took a deep breath and started planning a new running mix in her mind. She needed to add more Scissor Sisters. They always got her moving. "It's not the end of the season, Craig," she said, relaxing her shoulders. "It's January. In Minnesota. We can expect a few more months of ice."

Ignoring her like he always did when Elena or anyone tried to talk sense to him, Craig, in his puffy jacket and mom jeans, crouched down and peered at the bottom shelf. "*What* is this? What is *this*?" He held up a small box for Elena to see. It was a two-pack of waterproof sunscreen—not exactly a big seller this time of year.

"You going on a trip?" she asked. "To the tropics?"

"It's expired," Craig said.

Elena shrugged, suppressing an eye roll. "And?"

"And it's still on your shelves."

She let out a long, slow sigh, imagining herself slathering that expired sunscreen all over her arms and legs while lounging on a sandy beach somewhere far away from this guy in his late twenties who lived with his mom and had no apparent career prospects and therefore plenty of time to come into Elena's family's store and bug the crap out of her for hours on end. "What do you want me to do about it, Craig? Do you want the sunscreen for half off? You can have it for half off." At least that would count as a sale.

"I want you to care that it's there, Elena."

"*Motherfff…*" she hissed under her breath and turned toward the window, toward the Craig-free street outside. North Pole townies shuffled past the dilapidated Christmas trees and sun-faded plastic Santas on Main Street with hunched shoulders and scowls like they were prepared to murder the next person who offered them a cup of eggnog. Now that it was January, everyone in town was flat-out done with Christmas. The tourists had gone home, and it was time for the North Pole residents to resume their regular lives.

Elena spotted a line of about a dozen parka-clad people queuing up outside Prince's Sporting Goods across the street. "What's going on there?" Craig would know. Craig always knew.

She was right.

"Disgusting." He sneered, stepping toward the window. "Fickle little lemmings." He turned to face Elena again, about to launch into speech mode. "Do you see who's over there right now? Frank from the hardware store."

"Frank's there?" Elena squinted to see the line, searching for Frank, the owner of Santa's Workshop.

"He's not the only defector. We Coopers, however, chose Chestnut's Sporting Goods fifty years ago when the split happened, and we haven't patronized Prince's since."

"And we're very grateful for that." *And we'd be even more grateful if you'd freaking buy something once in a while.* Maybe Prince's would consider trading someone for Craig. But no, that would never happen. The Princes would never agree to anything that might help Chestnut's Sporting Goods.

Craig tossed the box of expired sunscreen up and down in his hand like a softball. "And now, just because the new Mr. Prince is offering deals on skates all week and he's having Stan Stashiuk in the store tomorrow for some big announcement and they're serving delicious free coffee to all their customers—"

Elena held up a hand to stop him. "Whoa, whoa, whoa. Wait a second. How do you know the coffee's delicious?"

Craig dropped the sunscreen. "Uh…"

"Craig?" Elena moved toward him.

"Someone told me!" he shouted, backing toward the door, arms raised in surrender.

"Who told you?" Elena's hands were fists.

"Dinesh."

"Dinesh?" Elena said. "He's one of our best customers!"

"It was definitely Dinesh."

Craig yanked the door open, but before he could leave, Elena said, "Hey, Craig?"

He turned around. "Yeah?"

"Thanks for stopping by." She grinned. Craig was a pain,

but he was her pain. And he had remained loyal to Chestnut's for years.

He waved. "Have a good one, Elena." Then he hurried out of the store, but not before shouting, "Make sure you get those expired products off the shelf!"

Elena's hand went right to the deadbolt. She could flip it so easily—one little motion and she wouldn't have to deal with Craig, or anyone else, for the rest of the day. Sighing, she let go of the lock and stepped away from the door. Her family needed the money, and Elena had to keep the store open for at least another three hours, even though Craig had probably been her last, best chance to sell anything at all today.

She picked up the sunscreen and carried it over to the summer supply aisle. Craig was right. A lot of this stuff was old—really old. Elena started taking all the expired items off the shelves—bug spray, lip balm, first aid supplies—and put everything in a big cardboard box marked "50% off." Then she went behind the counter and checked the clock.

Well, that had wasted a full fifteen minutes.

She grabbed a rag from the back room and started dusting everything in sight. Her parents did have a lot on their minds right now, but they had really let things go in the store. Or maybe it wasn't that. Maybe they had grown used to the people they'd hired doing the grunt work—like scrubbing bathrooms and stocking shelves. Maybe since they'd laid off all the regular workers, they'd forgotten they'd have to do the day-to-day cleaning and maintenance themselves.

Elena ran the rag across the tops of all the old photographs on the back wall behind the counter—pictures of her family going back three generations. Her grandfather, Marty Chestnut, had opened this store with his business partner, Robert Prince, back in 1962. Prince and Chestnut's, it was called then. But five years later, the two men got into a huge fight over money and split the store. Prince's moved across the street. Chestnut's stayed where it was. Her grandfather had put up a sign that said "We reserve the right to refuse service to any Prince." The town divided its loyalties between the two sporting goods stores, and both had managed to stay in business for more than fifty years.

Though for how much longer? The line outside Prince's had only grown in the past half hour, and Elena's store was a deserted wasteland.

She texted her best friend, Harper Anderson, and asked her to come by. The unflappably sunny Harper always provided a good distraction.

"I'll be right there," Harper replied.

Elena jumped on one of the floor-model treadmills facing the door, waiting for Harper, watching the queue outside Prince's. As the endorphins kicked in, she bumped her speed up a few notches. Then the door across the street opened and out came the son of the new owner—Oliver Prince. He was a junior like Elena, and he'd started at North Pole High School at the beginning of the year, but he wasn't around much. He didn't play sports or go to parties or anything. He was kind of invisible, an enigma with thick auburn hair and deep brown eyes.

As Oliver glanced at the line of people still waiting outside his family's store, he ran his fingers through that wavy, copper hair and plopped a green knit cap atop his head. Admittedly, Elena had thought he was cute at first, just like everyone had, until she'd found out he was a Prince. That had immediately brought him down from a nine to about a six.

The door opened behind Oliver and he spun around to hold it wide for his twin sister Regina—who had the same brown eyes and auburn hair, but behind glasses and with streaks of electric purple—and another girl, a short, buxom blonde Elena would recognize anywhere. Elena stumbled and nearly fell off the treadmill. Harper was hanging out with the Princes.

Elena regrouped and bumped up her speed another notch as punishment for her naïve disbelief. Harper had gone on the big ski trip with the Princes and most of the rest of their class over Christmas break. Elena hadn't been able to go because her parents couldn't afford it and because she had to help out in the store. According to the bits and pieces she'd heard from friends and the pictures she'd seen online, Elena had missed quite the epic time. And Harper had been acting weird and distant ever since, perhaps because she'd made friends with Elena's enemies and she didn't know how to break the news.

Harper, laughing, waved good-bye to the twins and skipped across the street. As she pulled open the door to Chestnut's, Elena fidgeted with the treadmill controls, hiding the fact that she'd been watching the window. She only glanced up when she heard the door shut behind Harper. She pressed the stop button and jogged until the belt stopped completely.

"Hey." Panting hard, Elena jumped off the treadmill. She smiled big, crushing the "What the hell were you doing with *them*?" question. Harper had the right to hang out with whomever she wanted.

Harper went right over to the sale stuff and started grabbing armfuls of expired sunscreen. She kept checking the window, glancing across the street to where the Princes were chatting animatedly in front of their store.

"That stuff's old," Elena said.

Again, Harper peered across the street. Clearly, she didn't want to be here at Chestnut's. She wanted to be across the street with the Princes and the delicious coffee and all the excitement. Not that Elena could blame her. All her parents' store had to offer was half off expired stuff no one would be able to use until June anyway.

Harper focused on Elena. "Spring break," she said, grinning. "Maybe it'll give me a better tan."

"Spring break?" Elena rang up her friend, trying to ignore Harper's puppy dog eyes and frequent peeks over at Prince's. "It's January. We literally just had winter break."

Harper leaned across the counter. "We're going to Florida. Captiva Island."

"We're?" asked Elena, bagging up the sunscreen.

Harper tapped Elena on the nose. "You and me, and my family, and maybe…some other people."

Elena guessed those "other people" included Oliver and Regina Prince. "I don't know if I'll be able to go," she said. "My parents need me—"

"They always need you," Harper said. "What about what you need? You need a fantastic vacation somewhere exotic."

Elena cocked a dubious eyebrow. "Like Florida?" Though she had to admit, Florida sounded pretty good right now. She wouldn't be up to her knees in slush there.

"Exactly." Harper grabbed a folder the Chestnuts kept next to the register, opened it, and started flipping through. "There's probably a race or something you can do down there that weekend, if that makes it more enticing—"

Elena snatched the folder back and shoved it into its usual spot. "Harper, I can't go. I'm busy."

"You are not." Harper waved her hand around the store. "This place is a ghost town. You dropped out of cross-country and track and field. You're not even tutoring anybody right now."

Elena swallowed. "I'm the only employee my parents have right now."

"Employee? Ha. Employees get paid. Your mom and dad have themselves, too. Where are they now? They should be here working, and you should be out there with me, being an irresponsible teenager. You missed such a great time over winter break." Harper's gaze traveled over to Prince's again. "I need you to be there for spring break. Promise me you'll come."

Elena sighed and glanced around the empty store. Saving enough money for the winter ski trip had been a bust. At this rate—with the store doing horribly and with Elena not bringing in any money tutoring—there was no way she'd be able to afford spring break. She couldn't tell Harper that, though. Harper's family had loads of money. If Harper found out Elena didn't have the funds, she'd pay for her trip in a minute. But friends and money didn't mix. She glanced up at the picture of her grandfather, Marty Chestnut, with his ex-friend and partner, Robert Prince. Her own family was living proof of that.

"I promise I'll try," Elena said finally.

. . .

"Oliver, stop worrying. You've done all you can at this point." His mom tossed her phone into her purse.

Oliver Prince balled and unballed his fists as he stared at the closed door to the Prince's Sporting Goods office where his twin sister, Regina, was hopefully putting the finishing touches on their grand plan, which they'd reveal to the town tomorrow evening.

He took a step toward the office. "I'm gonna check on her."

"Don't you dare." Oliver's dad, Trip Prince, who had just locked the front door of the store for the night, held up a hand to stop him. "She's in the zone."

Oliver sighed. His dad was out of his gourd. There was absolutely no chance that Regina was working her tail off behind that door right now, and not texting her friends or Snapchatting or whatever the hell else she did when Oliver needed her to get things done. While he had given up his own social life for the past six months, dedicating every free minute to working on this app for his dad, Regina had been out making friends and having a grand old time.

"It *has* to work tomorrow," Oliver said.

"It will." Oliver's mom guided him gently onto the stool behind the checkout counter. "Your sister always gets the job done, doesn't she? She always comes through in the end. She just goes about things differently than you do."

Oliver glowered. His mom had lawyered him, as she was wont to do. "Go back to Florida," he teased.

"Monday morning." Her eyes twinkling, his mom patted his shoulder. "Thank goodness. I can't take more than three days at a time in this frozen tundra."

Oliver's dad frowned. "So, you'll move here for good when the weather improves?"

She turned her back on Trip and poured herself a cup of hot water at the beverage bar the Princes had installed after the holidays. "How are things going for you, Oliver? Are you getting out, making friends?" She dropped an English Breakfast teabag into the mug.

"Yeah, I'm making friends," said Oliver.

His dad sauntered over to the coffee, poured himself a cup, and leaned against the beverage counter right next to his wife, who immediately shuffled a few steps to the side. "Oliver and Regina just went on a ski trip with a bunch of kids from school," Trip said. "Didn't you, Oliver?"

Oliver nodded, but he did not add that he'd only gone on the trip because Regina had dragged him along, or that he'd spent most of the vacation in the lodge lobby working on the game he was developing for his dad's store.

His mom pursed her lips, which meant he was about to get lawyered again. Jenny Prince, Esq., could sense bullshit from a mile away. "What did you do on this trip?"

"I hung out with people," Oliver said.

"Which people?" His mom folded her arms.

Which people? That was a good question, one with an answer his mother would find very unsatisfying. He uttered the first name that came to him. "Danny," he said. "Danny Garland."

"The coffee kid?" asked Mrs. Prince.

Oliver nodded. "The coffee kid." Danny's mom owned Santabucks, the café in town. They supplied the coffee for Prince's store, too. He was fine—kind of a jock, but fine.

"And what did you and the coffee kid do together on this trip?" When his mom sipped her tea, she looked like the toughest investigator in the grittiest procedural show on all of television.

"We skied?" Oliver shrugged, leaving his shoulders up by his ears a few beats too long.

"You skied?"

"Yup."

"You?" She placed her cup next to the cash register.

Oliver nodded, sweating under the store lights.

"You can't ski," his mom said, banging her hands on the counter.

"I brought my computer." Oliver raised his hands above his head. "I didn't want to go on the stupid trip, but Regina made me, and I sat in the lobby all week working on the app for the store. There." He wiped his brow.

Releasing Oliver like a witness she'd just put through the ringer, Mrs. Prince turned to her husband. "I trusted you to handle this."

"I'm handling it," said Trip, hangdog eyes on Oliver, who squirmed under his dad's gaze. He'd accidently made his dad look bad, something he'd been expressly asked not to do while his mom was in town. "This full-time parenting thing is new to me. I wasn't around as much in Florida with all the stores—"

"Now you have one store, Trip. One." She held up her index finger. "You sold the sandwich place, the burger joint, and the two chicken shacks. You've got more money than you know what to do with, and you have only this store to worry about."

"And two teenagers," said Trip. "This is why we need you here, Jenny."

"Dad's doing a great job, Mom," Oliver said.

His dad winked at him, and Oliver nodded in return. Sure, his dad hadn't made them a home-cooked meal in months, and sure, if Oliver and Regina wanted clean laundry, they had to take care of it themselves, but Oliver would never let his mom know that. He and his dad were allies. And besides, Oliver and his sister were practically adults anyway. They should be learning how to fend for themselves.

Shaking her head, Oliver's mom strolled to the window. She gazed outside for a moment, then turned around. "It's like back in Florida."

"It's nothing like Florida," joked Trip. "Have you been outside? It's negative ten degrees out."

Oliver chuckled. North Pole in January couldn't be more different than Orlando if it tried.

"That's not what I mean, and you know it." She pursed her lips. "I can't do everything, Trip. I just made partner. It's my turn to focus on my career."

"I know." He stepped toward her, and she took a step back. Oliver averted his eyes. In Florida, they'd always fight in private. But here they'd shown no qualms about airing their grievances in front of their kids. Yet another way North Pole was different.

"When we made this agreement—that you would sell the stores in Florida and take over your dad's shop here—you said you'd handle the stuff with the kids. You insisted that you'd have time to make sure Regina stayed out of trouble and that Oliver would keep his grades up, while branching out and making friends."

"Well, Regina has stayed out of trouble," said Trip. "Oliver's grades are fine, and he's hanging out with the coffee kid."

"Dad's right," Oliver said. "Regina's doing really well, and so am I."

His mom said, "No, you're not. Every time I'm in town, all you do is lock yourself in your bedroom or the office to play video games or work on that stupid app."

"It's not stupid," Oliver said.

"Maybe you're just here on the wrong weekends," Trip said. "Maybe if you were around more—"

Jenny Prince cocked her jaw for a moment, then, with her eyes on Oliver, said, "I want to see you expanding your horizons. Just a little. I'm not asking for much." She pointed to the window and Oliver followed her finger. Elena Chestnut was across the street, locking the door of her parents' store. "Get to know some people. Go out on a date. There's a cute girl right across the street."

Oliver chuckled. "That's not a cute girl. That's Elena Chestnut." The Chestnuts were the enemy. The Chestnut-Prince feud was legendary in North Pole, and Oliver's dad took it very seriously. The feud was the sort of thing that never came up in polite conversation around his parents and grandparents, and it had been enough to keep Oliver's dad away from North Pole for twenty years. His dad's sister, Aunt Becky, had brought it up once about ten years ago, but she'd been shut down swiftly and never invited to Thanksgiving again. Trip Prince did not half-ass his crusade against the Chestnut family, and neither did Oliver.

His mom shook her head. "You 'hate' the Chestnuts." She put "hate" in air-quotes. "You barely tolerate this town. Why did you even want to come back here, Trip?"

Oliver stared at the closed office door, willing it to open and for his sister to rush out and save the day, or at least to unlock the door and let him in.

"You know why," Trip said, not taking the bait.

Oliver's mom moved her hand like a mouth, imitating Trip. "'My dad died and I owed it to him to keep the store going.' Baloney. I know why you're here."

"Not now, Jenny," Trip muttered.

"He's here to defend his family's honor," said Oliver, repeating the party line. Trip leaned over and gave Oliver a high five.

"*Sic semper* Chesnuts," they said in unison. It was their anti-Chestnut rallying cry. In every bedtime story Trip told Oliver as a kid, there was always a monster named "Chestnut."

Regina opened the office door—too little, too late. Their parents had already stopped bickering. She triumphantly held up a large book. "Look what I found!" She opened it and started flipping through.

"You were supposed to be working in there." Oliver marched toward the office. "Do I have to do everything?"

"I was working, Oliver." Regina stopped on a specific page in the photo album and said, "But I also found this. You have to see Dad."

But before Regina could show her family the picture and before Oliver could sneak away, Trip Prince—whose face had gone completely white—yanked the book from his daughter's hands and quickly shut himself and the album inside the office.

"I was going to work in there." Oliver glared at the closed door.

"I guess you'll have to do something else instead." His mom wrapped a long, red scarf around her neck. "I'm heading back to the house. You should come, too. Or maybe call the coffee kid to hang out."

Itchy and tense, Oliver put on his own coat and gloves while gazing out the front door at the dark, oppressive cold.

The wind blew a torn Santa flag past the window. There was nothing to do in this stupid town. North Pole's motto was literally "Christmas 365 days a year!" Yes, with the exclamation point. It was Christmas at Christmas, Christmas in the summer, Christmas at Halloween and Thanksgiving. There was no escape. Oliver's computer was his only salvation. The game was his entire existence. Without it, he wouldn't survive the winter.

Chapter Two

Around five o'clock the next day, Elena realized that the only people she'd seen since breakfast were her parents. She'd opened Chestnut's at eleven, and her mom and dad showed up just before two. They were the first people to come through the doors that entire afternoon.

Her mom was now in the back room taking inventory. "Yell for me if things get crazy up front," she'd said.

Hahaha. Like that was going to happen. "Dad?"

He was behind the counter doing paperwork of some kind, his reading glasses falling toward the tip of his nose. "What is it, honey?"

"Um…" This subject had to be broached, but Elena wasn't sure how to do it. She understood the only real rule of engagement here was not to mention the name *Prince*. "So, I was thinking…what if we, you know, had an event in the store? Or maybe brought in, like, an expert to talk about skiing or…"

"This is about the Princes," her dad said, rubbing his temples.

"No," Elena said.

"Yes, it is. You heard about the things they're doing at the store now that Trip has taken over, and you're concerned about how it affects us."

"Well." Elena's shoulders dropped. "Yeah." *And I'm concerned I'll be working here every day of my life until I graduate high school, and that I'll never have the money to hang out with my friends, and on and on and on.*

"Don't be," her dad said. "Our store has been around for fifty years. We've seen lean times before. We'll get through this. It's January, after all. This is always the worst time of year for us."

Elena glanced around at the empty shop. He was right about that. Most of the North Pole stores suffered a bit after the holidays during the winter lull, when tourists went home, when no one in their right mind would want anything to do with a town whose sole reason for existence was to be a year-round Christmas tourist destination. But business had never been this lean before, at least not in recent memory, at least not to the point where her parents had to lay off all the superfluous workers (i.e. the workers they had to pay in actual money, not just room and board and familial guilt, like Elena). Usually they had a few locals a day coming in to buy supplies for skiing or hunting or hockey. But ever since the Princes starting doing whatever they were doing—providing massages and giving away gold bullion or who knows what—Chestnut's had been a ghost town.

"It seems worse this year, though," Elena said. There were other things, too, stuff beyond the store. Elena's mom had started clipping coupons, and Elena's dad had stopped going to the barbershop. He was letting his wife cut his hair instead. For as long as she could remember, her dad had loved getting his hair cut at Frosty's Dye and Trim. It was a huge bimonthly social event for him.

Her dad focused again on the bills in front of him. "You've been here too much, Elena. Why don't you take the afternoon off? Your mom and I will be fine."

His words were a brushoff. They were him telling her not to worry her little baby head about it, like he didn't think enough of her to be honest about the situation. She only wanted to help. She was as concerned as he was. As much as she resented being here at times, and as much as she imagined herself flitting off to deserted islands with sandy beaches, this store was her home-away-from-home, too.

She grabbed her parka and stepped outside, where the December scent of roasted nuts and cinnamon had been replaced by January's car exhaust and dirty slush. If "grime" had a specific odor, this was it. The yoga studio next door, Om Holy Night, still had a plastic reindeer decorating their doorstep. Glancing around, Elena checked to make sure no one was watching her. Then she kicked Rudolph onto his side, but she righted him before pulling out her phone to text Harper. Maybe they could meet for coffee at Santabucks or for dinner at Mags's Diner.

But the pit in Elena's gut told her she already knew what Harper was up to. She was at Prince's right now, waiting to hear whatever big announcement Stan Stashiuk was about to make, probably fawning all over Oliver Prince and his sister. Gross.

Elena glanced back to make sure her dad wasn't watching, then she put her hood up, crossed the street, and opened the front door of the enemy's shop.

She didn't need the hood. No one rubbernecked toward the door when she came in. No one even noticed she was there. The entire place was crammed wall-to-wall with townspeople, people she'd known her entire life. There were the folks who had always been loyal to Prince's, of course, but there were Chestnut's regulars as well—like Craig, Dinesh Chahuan, and

Danny Garland. He was in her class at school, and she had known him since she was born. He and his girlfriend, Star Lyons, were standing next to the coffee machine, which was almost too much to take.

Elena pushed her way over to Danny and slapped his shoulder, a move which no doubt hardly permeated his thick, down jacket. "You're standing next to the free coffee bar. You." She poked him in the chest. "Your mom owns the coffee shop."

Danny shot Star a side-eye. "Um…hi, Elena."

Star gave her a bored nod, and flipped her long, blond braid across her shoulder.

"Hi," Elena said, staring pointedly at the coffee.

"My mom…sold them the coffee…" Wincing, he played with the zipper of his jacket.

Elena's jaw dropped.

"It was a business thing," he explained. "Trip came in and offered her a bunch of money to supply coffee for the store…"

Elena's jaw dropped further.

"It's…just business," Danny said again.

"*Traitor*," Elena hissed. She marched back toward the front of the store, about to leave and tell her parents how everyone in this town was a lying piece of garbage, but then the mayor, Cesar Sandoval, took the stage and asked for quiet. The crowd grew silent almost on cue. If she opened the door, the jingling of the stupid Christmas bells would draw all focus to her. Instead, she ducked behind a rack of ski parkas.

"Welcome to the new Prince's!" Mayor Sandoval said, and everyone but Elena started clapping. She spotted Harper up near the riser at the front of the store where the mayor was standing, towering over everyone else in the room. Next to Harper was Regina Prince. Regina was talking to Stan Stashiuk, the hockey player, and Harper was leaning across Regina, trying to shoehorn herself into their conversation.

"I am honored that Trip has asked me to be the one to announce this wonderful contest he has organized with the help of one of North Pole's favorite sons, Stan Stashiuk. Come on up, Stash!"

Stan Stashiuk clambered onto the riser and stood next to the mayor. Elena, of course, knew Stash, but mostly by reputation. He was about three years older than she was, and had left North Pole right after high school to play hockey like his dad, who was from Poland. Stash was tall and broad with a curly-frizzy man bun, and he looked like he needed time to grow into his face, which he had gotten from his mother, a model from Ghana. The big difference between Stash and his mom, however, was that his mouth was currently missing two teeth.

The mayor handed Stash the microphone. "My family has always been Team Prince," Stash said.

Elena groaned. "Barf."

Stash continued. "My parents and I are glad to see Trip continuing tradition and keeping Prince's Sporting Goods in the family. In honor of the grand reopening, Trip and I and his kids, Regina"—Regina shot Stash a dazzling smile as he continued speaking—"and Oliver, who is...somewhere, created a competition we're calling Stash Grab. How many of you played Pokémon GO last summer?"

A few people raised their hands. Craig and Dinesh clapped enthusiastically, but Elena shook her head. Traitors.

"This game is a little like that. There are virtual Stashes all over town. If you download the app and walk around, they'll pop up on your screen. Answer the question, capture the Stash, get the points. Whoever winds up with the most points at the end of the game gets the grand prize—a $200 gift card to Prince's, a jersey signed by me, and two round-trip tickets to anywhere in the continental U.S., provided by my sponsor, Bronze Airlines—Go for the Bronze!" Rolling his eyes, he stuck an unenthusiastic fist in the air and handed the mic back to Mayor Sandoval before scrambling off the stage to Regina, who giggled and whispered in his ear.

Elena groaned. What a sucky prize—two hundred bucks to Prince's Sporting Goods. Of course, the airline tickets wouldn't be a bad thing. She could even use those for spring break. And she could probably sell the jersey somewhere online for spending money. Ugh, was she actually talking herself into playing this game? *No. Stop it, Elena.*

A voice from behind her whispered, "Scouting the competition?"

She spun around, nearly knocking over the rack of jackets. Oliver Prince was sitting behind her on the ground, his back against the wall. He had a laptop on his thighs, and his brown eyes were focused hard on whatever was on the screen.

"No." She folded her arms and turned back toward the stage.

"Big Stash fan?"

She didn't answer him. The mayor was talking again, laying out the rules and regulations for the game.

"You probably don't want this, then?"

She turned around, and he, eyes and one hand still on the computer, was holding out a bright green flier. She saw the words "Stash Grab" in big block letters right in the middle of the page.

"Nope." She turned back around. "You're right. I don't want that."

"Suit yourself," he said. "Your dad might, though. Just to see what a successful business does to stay profitable."

She spun on her heel. "Eat a bag of hockey pucks," she hissed, and marched out of the store.

• • •

As he got dressed for school, Oliver's brain ticked through everything he needed to remember about the game. He and Regina had set up the Stashes to come and go at varying intervals, kind of like blinking Christmas lights. All the questions were ready to be doled out over the course of the next two months, thanks to his sister. She was the one who'd done all the extensive Stan Stashiuk research. Oliver had created an automated sign-up, so there was nothing to do there.

Everything was ready to go, and the game would probably run smoothly. There was no reason it wouldn't. But he couldn't shake the feeling that he needed to be on the computer at all times, monitoring everything, defeating any potential bugs— or not bugs, gnats. Tiny little hiccups. He'd ensured there'd be no screw-up bigger than that.

In the kitchen, his mom poured coffee into a travel mug.

"What time's your flight back to Florida?" he asked. Not that he wanted her to leave or anything, though it would be nice not to have someone looking at her watch every time he sat down to play Wizard War.

"I pushed it," she said. "I'm leaving later tonight."

Oliver scooped scrambled eggs onto his plate and grabbed a banana.

His mom tested her coffee and then screwed the lid on tight. "Your dad and I are going to school with you this morning."

Oliver's banana fell to the ground.

"We want to have a chat with the principal."

Oliver took a seat at the table. He shoved a big forkful of eggs into his mouth, but he couldn't taste anything. This wasn't going to be good. His mom had met several times with his principal back in Florida. Every time, she said the same thing—Oliver needed to branch out, put down the computer. Every time, his dad had saved him, reminding everyone that computers were Oliver's lifeblood. He wasn't like other kids who played sports and hung out doing...whatever. He designed games. Playing video games wasn't a waste of time for Oliver. It was research.

But Oliver got the distinct feeling his dad's support wasn't going to be worth much this time around.

He and his parents said good-bye to Regina at the front door of the high school. She mouthed "Good luck" to Oliver before falling into step with some of her girlfriends. He envied her sometimes, her ability to do it all. She wasn't as talented as Oliver computer-wise, but she was good enough. And she was popular. She got decent grades. She always had something to do on Friday night, someone to sit with at lunch.

It wasn't that he cared for himself that he didn't have those things. But succeeding in at least one area outside of gaming might get his mom off his back.

As he and his parents marched through the halls toward the principal's office, Oliver scanned the crowd. People everywhere had their heads down on their phones. He grinned when he heard someone shout, "There's a Stash right here!" A stampede of students charged over to the drinking fountain, their fingers moving deftly across their screens.

Harper's brother Sam, a senior, waved to Oliver. "Great game, Oliver!"

Oliver's heart sped up and his face flushed. No one had ever shouted his name across a crowded hallway before. That better reflected Regina's high school experience.

"I don't see anything," Oliver's mom said, craning her neck. "The kid says there was a Stash. Where's the Stash?"

Oliver rolled his eyes. How very *mom* of her. "It's a virtual Stash. When you have the app open, it shows a rough landscape of where we are. Then—pop!—a Stash shows up on-screen. Then you click on it and answer a question. If you get the question right, you get the points. The harder the question, the more points the Stash is worth."

"It's pretty genius," said Trip.

Again, Oliver's cheeks burned hot.

His mom was still staring at the drinking fountain. "So they have to keep the app open at all times."

Oliver grinned. "If they want to win they do."

His mom shook her head. "It seems like a colossal waste of time."

"Ouch," whispered Oliver.

"Not for us." His dad put an arm around Oliver's shoulders. "Every so often, a coupon for a flash sale at Prince's will pop up."

"And we have some really valuable Stashes in the store," Oliver added. At least his dad was on his side.

His mom watched as a freshman girl crashed right into a locker because her eyes were down on her phone. "Whatever you say." She pulled open the door to the principal's office, which was still dripping with garland from Christmas.

The three Princes sat across the desk from the principal, Mrs. Olsen. Oliver noticed that she, too, had her phone open to the Stash Grab app. Everyone was getting involved. He had never been prouder of anything in his entire life, though a sour pit in his stomach was harshing his buzz. This meeting wasn't going to end well.

Mrs. Olsen passed a sheet of paper across her desk. Oliver's mom picked it up. "After you called," Mrs. Olsen said, "I printed off Oliver's grades just to see how he's been doing. I haven't had any specific complaints from teachers, but I did notice a few things." She reached over and pointed to a spot near the bottom of the page. "He has zero extracurriculars. Zero. That's not good."

"He's been working on the game," said Mr. Prince.

The principal nodded. "That's very impressive, but it's rather limiting. We like to see our students a little more well-rounded, of course."

"Of course," said his mom.

"Oliver's grades are average, for the most part, which is fine, but I have a feeling he can do better."

His mom scanned the page in front of her with wide eyes. "I know he can." She put the paper down, took off her glasses, and stared at him. "You, of all people, should not have a C in math."

Yes, he absolutely should have a C in math. He never did his homework, and he sat in the back of class avoiding the teacher's eyes. A C wasn't too shabby, all things considered.

"I'm more concerned about the Latin grade, honestly." Mrs. Olsen highlighted a box in the middle of the page. "I know he can pull up his numbers in math and science, and in social studies and English, classes that are less cumulative. If he starts working harder now in those subjects, he'll be fine." She pointed to the Latin grade, which was currently a C- and dropping. "His Latin grade keeps falling, and I'm concerned that he's so far behind now, he won't be able to pull the grade up on his own."

"And he definitely won't be able to improve any of these scores if he keeps playing around on the computer." His mom scribbled notes on a legal pad.

Mrs. Olsen nodded.

Oliver's mom glared at his dad. "You see this, right? Tell me I'm not the only one who sees this."

Trip stared at the progress report. "You're not the only one."

"So, what are we going to do about it?" Oliver's mom bit her lip.

"We can cut back on his computer ti—"

Oliver shook his head. *No. No cutting back on computer time.*

"We tried that, Trip. Remember? Last year? We tried

enforcing time limits, and it didn't work. His grades didn't improve. And you kept caving when he asked you nicely. I need to know that you're on my side here. Please, Trip. We have to be a team." She ran her fingers through her hair, then turned to Oliver. "I understand that you love what you do with the games and all of it. I get that. Don't think I don't. But, honey." She pointed to the grades. "This is unacceptable. You're limiting yourself in so many ways. You need to get out and make friends."

"I have friends." He had Regina and…Regina's friends.

"You don't."

"I like my life." Yeah, things got a little pathetic and gloomy at times, but he was happy being a lone wolf. He didn't have to answer to anyone but himself. He didn't have to worry about his classmates rejecting him because he wasn't the funniest or the best at small talk. He was awkward around other people. It was easier for him to keep to himself. He liked keeping to himself.

His mom closed her eyes for a moment. "I want more for you, Oliver. But at the very least, I want you to start taking school seriously. Because with these grades, you're not going to a great college. You're not. And you want that, don't you?"

"I always figured my skills would be enough." He did one thing and he did it well. Why did he have to be a Renaissance man?

The principal shook her head. "They won't be. Not when you're competing against thousands of other kids with the same abilities, but who also get better grades and participate in extracurricular activities."

He sighed. Maybe she was right. What could it hurt to do a bit more homework and maybe join, like, the chess club or something? There had to be some club at school that wouldn't be abject torture. "Fine. I will work less on the computer stuff. Regina can do more for the game. I mean, it's mostly down to her questions and placing the Stashes anyw—"

His mom shook her head. "That's not going to fix it. It's not going to be enough." She held out her hand. "Hand me your laptop."

"What?"

"Give it to me."

With a lump in his throat, he pulled his computer out of his bag and handed it to his mom. He stared at his dad, waiting for Trip to argue his son's case. He didn't.

His mom handed the laptop to Trip. "Your dad will hold onto this until you bring your grades up and start socializing more." She turned to her husband. "I'm counting on you here. You're the main parent right now. Hide his tablet. Change the passwords on the computers at home and at the office— Regina's, too. I don't want him working on the Stash Grab game at all. For the next few months, he's going cold turkey." His mom frowned. "It's for your own good, Oliver. Honey, you need a break."

Oliver glanced out the window to the hallway, where students were filing past. This was completely unfair. The game was his baby, and she was asking him to cede control to Regina, of all people? She had too many other things going on in her life. The entire game would fall apart with her in charge. He couldn't let that happen. His dad had to know that. He had to know how dire the situation would be without Oliver in charge.

He exhaled. He'd say yes now and then find a way to get his stuff back. His dad would cave, of course he would. His dad was on his team. And Mom would be back in Florida by tonight. "Okay," Oliver said. "It's a deal."

Chapter Three

Six people bumped into Elena on the way to first period Monday morning. They all had their eyes on their phones while trying to navigate the halls of North Pole High School.

When number six, a freshman boy who only came up to Elena's shoulder, ran straight into her back, she spun around and grabbed his arm. "What is going on?"

"Stash Grab," he said, like, *duh, who didn't know that*?

"That stupid Stan Stashiuk game?"

"It's not stupid," he said. "Two hundred bucks can go a long way at Prince's."

Elena blinked. "Wait. You're Jimmy Shaw."

He nodded.

She shook his arm. "Your family has been shopping at Chestnut's for years."

"You gonna give me two hundred bucks to shop at your store?"

Elena's jaw dropped, and she let him go. He immediately ran right into the nearest locker.

In her first class, social studies, everyone bombarded

Oliver Prince with questions, even the teacher.

Ms. White sat on the edge of her desk, eyes trained on Oliver in the front row, two seats over from Elena. "How far out do they go? I mean, like, are there Stashes out at Wal-Mart?"

Oliver sighed as if his entire world was ending. Even his usually glorious auburn hair seemed less shiny and luxurious today. Poor baby. "The Stashes are inside town limits only. They're as far south as Poinsettia Place, as far west as Evergreen Street, as far north as Jasmine Terrace, and as far east as Cedar street. The golf resort is also fair game. So's the ski resort."

Their teacher nodded slowly, taking this in. "And there are going to be more Stashes over the next few weeks?"

"They're on a timer, a clock." Oliver fidgeted, shifting in his seat like he wasn't used to the attention and he'd given this same spiel at least a hundred times over the past few hours. "Stashes come and go at varying intervals. If the app is open and the GPS tracker knows you're in the area, the Stash pops up at the right time. The harder ones, the ones with more difficult questions that only pop up every few days or so, are worth more points. The ones that are around a lot—"

"And have easy questions like Stash's middle name?" asked Ms. White.

"Right," Oliver said. "Those are worth less, but you can collect them as many times as you see them. Once you grab that Stash—or even try to answer the question—it's gone until the timer releases it again."

The teacher nodded her head, stood up, and went to the board. Elena opened her social studies notebook and aimed her pen at the blank page, ready for class to begin finally, but Ms. White said, "Okay, everyone, let's share. Where have you found Stashes around town? I'll start. There's one in the frozen foods section at Ludlum's Grocery Store." She wrote this on the board, while hands shot up all over the room.

Elena groaned. Oliver turned toward her, frowning.

"I'd like to, you know, *learn* something," she whispered across the girl between them, Marley Ho, who was furiously writing down every place on the board.

Oliver hissed, "Yeah, so would I," before facing front again.

Before lunch, Elena met Harper at her locker, like usual; but Harper flew right past Elena, eyes down on her phone.

"Not you, too," Elena shouted, her hands balled up in frustration.

Harper swung around, but she didn't put her phone away. "'Me, too,' what?"

"That stupid game." Elena's finger jabbed toward Harper's hand.

Taking a step toward Elena, Harper glanced down at her phone. "Yeah, and?"

"You hate hockey. It's one of the first things we bonded over. We're, like, the only two girls in North Pole who can't stand stinking hockey."

"That hasn't changed." Harper took a quick glance at her phone, realized what she was doing, and then stared intently at Elena. "I like to win. You know that. Remember the Sugarplum Sweethearts?" Harper had entered the town beauty queen competition two years in a row, and never made it past the first round. Elena had consoled her friend both times with under-baked chocolate chip cookies made from store-bought dough—their favorite.

"True, but why even bother entering? It's not like you need the money. You can buy your own plane ticket, and you don't even shop at Prince's. What are you going to do with a two-hundred-dollar gift card to their store?"

"Flush it down the toilet?" Harper jumped as her phone buzzed. "There's one in the girls' bathroom!" she hissed, eyes darting around, making sure no one else had heard her.

Elena trailed into the bathroom after her friend. Harper had never moved this fast in her life. Elena was the runner.

Harper skidded to a stop near the sinks and pressed a few buttons on her phone. "How many hat tricks did Stash get during his rookie year?" Looking somewhere between panicked and utterly confounded, she frowned in the mirror at Elena. "I hate it when they ask about stats. I never know any of them. And you only have twenty seconds to answer."

"It's four," said Elena.

Harper's mouth dropped open as she typed the answer and pressed enter. A few seconds later, she said, "Hmph."

"I got it right?"

"Yeah," said Harper. "How the hell did you know that?"

"My parents own a sporting goods store. You pick things up."

Elena watched her friend in the mirror. Harper's eyes were still on her phone. "You should play this game," Harper said.

"Yeah, right."

"I'm serious. You know loads about Stash and town history and gossip. There are some North Pole-centric questions, too." Harper glanced up at Elena, her eyes wide. "You could win the tickets. For spring break."

"Ugh." It wasn't like the thought hadn't occurred to her. Florida sounded so, so good to her right now. A fun spring break, lying on the beach with her best friend, would be amazing.

"You're interested."

"No, I'm not." Elena tucked her long, wavy hair behind her ears, avoiding Harper's gaze in the mirror. "It's a ridiculous game, and you shouldn't be playing it because the Princes are vile."

"But I want to play it."

"Again," said Elena, eyes now on Harper, "why? You don't need the money. You don't want a Stan Stashiuk jersey."

Harper blushed slightly.

And Elena caught on. Oh. Of course. It wasn't the game at all. "It's not about Stash, is it? Or the money."

Harper shook her head.

"What's it about, then?" But the answer was obvious. She and Harper had been best friends, inseparable best friends, for five years. Harper had a crush. "You like someone."

Harper's jaw dropped. "How did you—?"

"I can tell." Elena gazed into her best friend's eyes like a fortuneteller, searching for more information. "You like... someone having something to do with Stash Grab...someone you don't want me to know about." She paused. "Ugh. It's Oliver Prince." She mimed vomiting.

"No, it's not," said Harper.

"Please. Who else could it be?" Of course Elena's best friend liked the bane of her existence. The universe was just that cruel.

Harper opened her mouth to protest further, but then her shoulders slumped. "Okay, yeah. It's him."

"I know you better than anyone." Elena's shoulders sank. "I can tell when you have a crush. Why didn't you tell me?" They told each other everything. Or, they used to.

Harper opened her mouth again, but Elena stopped her. "It's because of the feud thing, isn't it?"

"Yeah, that's it," said Harper, quickly.

Elena squinted. There was still more Harper wasn't saying. "Does he like you?"

Harper sighed, staring at the florescent light above her. "I thought so. If you had asked me a few weeks ago, I would've said yes."

"This has been going on for a few weeks?"

"Since the ski trip over break. Or really, stuff happened

while on the trip, but ever since then—" Now Harper actually did start crying.

Harper had never been this broken up over a guy, and there had been a lot of guys. It always inspired the heck out of Elena to see how tough Harper was around her various boyfriends, and how cool. She was the kind of girl who stayed friends with every one of her exes, which was probably some form of self-preservation, since they lived in such a small town. When things went south between Harper and one of her boyfriends, they had a mature discussion over lattes at Santabucks and then went their separate ways. There were no tears. There was no yelling. There was no drama.

Elena wrapped her friend in a massive bear hug. "Why didn't you tell me? We could've been commiserating for weeks over this jerk. Imagine all the pints of ice cream we could've consumed. So much wasted ice cream time." She held Harper at arm's length. "Were you afraid of making me feel bad? Because of the feud?"

Harper nodded. "That's totally why."

Elena peered at her again, trying to read Harper. She was still hiding something. But since Elena hadn't yet said anything to her about how Chestnut's was about to go under, she couldn't judge Harper's need for some privacy. "You know you can tell me anything."

Harper nodded.

"I'm not just saying that."

"I know," said Harper.

"Did something…happen…on the ski trip? Something bad?" If that Oliver Prince asshole had hurt Harper…

Harper shook her head. "Nothing bad. Just stuff I'm trying to work out for myself, you know?"

"I get that." Elena frowned. What could possibly be so big or so bad that Harper would need to keep it this far under wraps? "But please know I'm here for you. No matter what."

"Thank you," said Harper. "That means a lot. Especially because of the feud thing."

"Don't even worry about that." Elena leaned over to hug her friend again, but Harper swung up her arm with the phone, knocking Elena right in the jaw.

"There's another Stash right outside!"

Harper rushed out the bathroom door, and Elena followed her, massaging her wounded chin. She was fighting a losing battle against Stash Grab and the Prince family.

The rest of the day was more of the same. Everywhere Elena went, the people she encountered were consumed by Stash fever. Before the start of eighth period, Katie Murphy, who worked in the principal's office during her free period, handed Elena a note. "Mrs. Olsen wants to see you."

A swirling sickness in her gut, Elena headed down to the principal's office. It was never a good thing when the principal wanted to see you, was it? Not that she could remember doing anything wrong. Maybe she was going to be chastised for not playing Stash Grab like the rest of the sheeple in town.

Speaking of, Mrs. Olsen had the app open on her phone, which was sitting on her desk. She closed it when she saw Elena staring. "My son," she explained. "He needs new skis."

Elena shrugged. It was fine. The Olsens had always shopped at Prince's anyway. They weren't traitors like that Jimmy Shaw.

"Are you still interested in tutoring?" Mrs. Olsen said.

"Yeah," Elena said immediately. "I've been waiting for the call all year. I will tutor anyone in any subject."

"Fantastic, and I'll ask you to remember that sentiment when you see who's looking for help." Mrs. Olsen pushed a sealed envelope across her desk. "While math tutors are a dime a dozen, there aren't a lot of options for people who need assistance in Latin. This young gentleman's grades are slipping, but with some help, I know he can bring them up.

His parents are desperate." She coughed. "Really desperate. They'll pay you twenty-five dollars per session, plus a hundred if you can raise his grade to a B, and another two hundred for an A."

"Wow," Elena said, starting to open the envelope. "They're serious."

"And they'd like you to start as soon as possible, you know, assuming you want the job."

Elena frowned. "Of course I want the job."

"You say that now." Mrs. Olsen furrowed her brow. "How about tomorrow after school?"

Elena started to say "That's fine," but she stopped when she pulled the name out of the envelope. She was going to be tutoring Oliver Prince.

• • •

Elena snapped her fingers in front of Oliver's face. "The seven kings. Who were they?"

He sighed, slowly dragging his eyes away from the Santabucks window. He was not about to jump to attention just because it was what Elena Chestnut wanted him to do. The world on Main Street outside was much more interesting, anyway. Several of his fellow students—and a few of North Pole's adult residents—were dashing through the snow, trampling decrepit, months-old Santa hats and Christmas wreaths, frantically catching Stashes. "I don't know who the seven kings were," he said. "Isn't that why you're tutoring me?"

"I want to be here as much as you do." Elena's brown eyes were hard, unflinching. She had put her long, dark hair up in a bun, which was held in place by a pencil. "I'm only tutoring you because your parents are paying me. I'm not doing this for my health."

"At least you're getting paid." Oliver let his eyes drift again to Main Street outside. The little old lady who owned the diner on the edge of town—Mags Something-or-other—was jumping up and down over catching a Stash. The red ball of her stocking cap slapped her in the face. He, Oliver, had made that happen. He'd inspired an elderly woman to risk breaking a hip on an icy sidewalk. But he was being forced to give up control of his creation.

Elena handed him a stack of blank index cards. "Yeah, and the better you do, the more money I make. What do you get?"

He glared at her. "I get my life back."

She frowned like she was tempted to ask him more about this, but she didn't. Oliver gave her credit for that. "So," she said, "this next quiz is as good a chance as you're going to get to do that." She opened the textbook in front of her. "It's all history, no translation. There will be no Latin on the Latin quiz. Magister Parker just wants to make sure we have the background down before we start translating Livy's words. What do you know about the kings of Rome?"

Oliver shrugged and folded his arms. "You're the tutor. Shouldn't you tell me? This would go a lot easier if you just gave me the answers."

She sucked in a deep, calming breath of air, like she was trying to keep it together. "You'll learn nothing if I feed you the answers." She tapped on one of the notecards in front of him. "Write 'Romulus' on this side."

Oliver rolled his eyes. This was such a waste of time. There were so many other things, better things, he could be doing right now. "You know, you don't have to sit here with me. I am fully capable of learning this on my own."

"Your grades and the fact that your parents felt the need to hire me as a Latin tutor would suggest otherwise." She tapped her pencil on the notecards again. "And after you write 'Romulus' on this side, take out your notes from class today and write everything you know about him on the back."

"I didn't take any notes. And I don't have a pen."

Elena pulled the pencil out of her bun and tossed it at his chest. Her long, dark waves cascaded around her shoulders and her eyes flashed savagely, like she could eat Oliver alive and enjoy doing it. He, however, was saved by an actual bell when his sister, Stan Stashiuk, and Harper Anderson entered Santabucks.

Grinning, Regina and her entourage sauntered over to his table. "Hey, Ollie. On a date?" Then she noticed who the girl sitting across from him was. "With Elena Chestnut?"

"She's tutoring me." He scratched the name "Romulus" onto the back of his notecard.

"Your parents are paying me to be in his presence," Elena said, "otherwise I'd be absolutely anywhere else."

While Stash went up to the counter to grab drinks, Harper took the chair next to Elena and rested her head on her friend's shoulder. "You're helping him with Latin?"

"I'm trying to," Elena said, glaring once again at Oliver. On anyone else, those burning brown eyes would be enticing, but on Elena Chestnut, they were grotesque. She was like a monster, a gorgon. How was that for a classical reference, Ms. Tutor?

"Do Mom and Dad know she's the one tutoring you?" Regina asked. She locked eyes with Elena. "No offense or anything, they just…"

"Don't like my family," Elena said.

Regina winced. "Putting it mildly."

"They were not happy about the situation, but they felt"— Oliver waved his hand up and down to indicate Elena—"was their last resort." Actually, his dad had tried to put his foot down, but Oliver's mom had overpowered him. She'd said, "What does it matter to you if the Chestnut girl is the one helping Oliver? Is there any reason why that would make you *uncomfortable*?" The way she said the word "uncomfortable" appeared to have been the last straw for Oliver's dad. Trip had signed off immediately on Elena as Oliver's tutor.

"Elena's really smart," Harper said. "You're in good hands."

"But I can't work miracles," Elena said.

Oliver watched his sister, who waved at Stash as he dumped a mound of sugar into his coffee. What had she been doing since school let out an hour ago? Had she checked up on the game? Was she here to interview Stash for more questions? Oliver tried to play it cool. "How's it…going?" he asked.

Regina raised an eyebrow as she took a cup from Stan Stashiuk. "How's it…going?" She sipped her coffee. The way she did that was infuriating. It was the same "grizzled detective" way their mom sipped her tea. "It's going. We're picking up some stuff from Harper's for Stash Cares."

"Stash Cares?" Elena asked.

Who cares? Oliver thought. He wanted to be talking about the game, not about whatever Stan Stashiuk was up to.

"It's my foundation." Stash checked the lid on his coffee. "Kind of a big brother/big sister thing that uses sports to reach out to Minnesota kids in poverty, but particularly the Somali youth in and around the Twin Cities."

"Stash is using hockey to save the world." Regina beamed up at Stash the way Oliver used to gaze at his computer. "He uses a huge chunk of his endorsement money to fund the charity."

"Go for the Bronze," Stash said, rolling his eyes.

Regina giggled and nudged him in the side.

"And my dad is donating a bunch of basketball equipment," Harper said. "That's what we're dealing with today."

"Okay." Oliver winced. He could be such a dick sometimes. "That's, like, legitimately awesome, Stash. If you need any more help, let me know."

"Me, too," Elena added. "Maybe Chestnut's can donate some stuff."

"I know Prince's definitely can," Oliver said. Elena Chestnut would not one-up him on this. "Just let us know how we can help." Then he asked Regina, "And how's the game going?" He shrugged, hoping to give the appearance that he couldn't care less how things were playing out, like it didn't matter to him at all that he had been banished from monitoring his creation.

Regina shook her head. "I'm not getting in the middle of this. Mom and Dad put me in charge, and I've got it. I can handle it. Your part was done anyway. I'm just placing Stashes and coming up with questions." She nodded toward Stan Stashiuk. "Your job now is to get your grades up."

Oliver clasped his hands together. He would've gotten down on his knees if he weren't in the middle of a coffee shop. "Just keep me in the loop. Please."

She shook her head. "I'm not trying to be an asshole, but I am trying to stay on Mom's good side. I'm the angel for once." She grinned, sticking a finger in her dimple. "And you, buddy, here's the perfect chance to expand your horizons, make some new friends." She nodded to Harper and Stash. "Let's give these two some room."

The three of them left for Harper's house, while Oliver remained in Santabucks with Elena Chestnut and a bunch of dead monarchs.

Elena pointed again to the index card. "Romulus," she said. "Do you want me to spell it?"

"Bite me," he said.

She leaned back in her chair and tied her hair back up in that bun. "Oh no, no, no, my friend. Your entire existence, Oliver Prince, rests in my hands." She nodded toward the table. "I think, from now on, you'll do as I say."

Chapter Four

"Are you going to buy anything, Craig?" Elena shouted as he opened the door to leave Chestnut's.

Craig turned around, phone in hand, the infernal Stash Grab music blasting from his headphones. He pulled out his earbuds to speak to Elena. "Uh…I'll be back," he said.

"Sure you will," Elena shouted from behind the cash register. "Sure, you'll be back. Once this stupid game is over." She hurled a foam football from the impulse buy bin on the counter. Craig escaped through the front door before it could hit him.

This had been happening all day. Some evil, sadistic member of the Prince family—that jerk Oliver, no doubt, angry at her for making him learn things—had put a Stash inside Chestnut's, right next to their ski display. People had been filing into the store in a near-constant stream, pretending to shop while really waiting for the Stash to reappear. Mayor Sandoval had come in, and Marley Ho and Danny Garland and Star Lyons. Harper and Ms. White had stopped by. Ms. White had bought a tube of lip balm, at least. A sixty-five-cent thing of lip balm. That was the only sale Elena had made all day.

And, to add insult to injury, she actually knew the answer to the dumb question in her store: What was the middle name of Stan Stashiuk's great-grandfather, Steven? The answer was "Gregory," same name as Stash's dog. She knew that because her grandmother, before she died, used to run a pet grooming service out of her house. Stan Stashiuk had been one of her customers. It was like the game itself was taunting her—*You should be playing, Elena. You could be winning.*

When the question popped up again an hour later, she was not alone in the store. Dinesh was there, pretending to examine the ski boots. So were a few kids from school—freshmen—and a couple other locals. Frank, who owned Santa's Workshop, the hardware store, didn't even pretend like he was doing anything but hunting Stashes. He just stood in a corner, in his overalls and red and green plaid flannel, watching his phone. Dolores Page, the sweet old lady who washed linens for the church, hovered near Elena at the counter.

"Are you playing, Dolores?" Elena asked.

"You betcha," said Dolores, eyes down on her phone.

"You have a smartphone?" Elena tried to remember which birthday the town had recently celebrated for Dolores. Was it eighty or eighty-one?

With a withering air, Dolores glanced up at Elena. "Of course I own a smartphone."

"It's here!" shouted Dinesh.

Everyone in the store opened their apps and tried frantically to catch the Stash. Frank got it right away and ducked quickly out of Chestnut's. Dolores was only a few seconds behind him. Dinesh, a few beats after her.

The freshmen stared at their phones, dumbfounded, the poor babies. "You don't know the answer?" Elena asked.

"No," said one of them, a girl. *Probably one of the Joyce kids*, Elena thought, because the girl was wearing one of the moth-ridden Christmas sweaters the family sported all winter long—from November until deep into March. "Do you know it?"

Elena hesitated. What was it to her if she gave away the answer? She wasn't playing. Plus, it could be a good marketing strategy—community outreach to make people feel more loyal toward her store. *Come to Chestnut's! They're nice there and they'll give you Stash Grab answers.*

"It's Gregory," she said, seeking nothing in return. This was her good deed for the day.

"Cool!" said the Joyce girl, before she and the rest of the kids stormed toward the exit.

"Where are you going?" Elena shouted.

"This Stash won't be back for an hour at least," the Joyce girl said. "We're off to find others." They dashed across the street, nearly getting taken out by Sam Anderson's rusted-out pickup truck.

"Ingrates," Elena mumbled.

It was January, close to ten below with the wind chill, but Main Street was crawling with North Pole townies. They were everywhere—standing in front of fire hydrants, hovering in stairwells, checking out gangways. There were more people on the street today than on any gorgeous day in summer. Craig Cooper high-fived Dottie, the girl with the bright red hair who worked in the bakery. Kevin Snow gave Dinesh a noogie on his head. People hurried up and down the street with hot chocolate and apple cider sloshing onto their mittens. They were having fun. They were acting like a community.

And Elena was stuck inside this empty store with one virtual Stan Stashiuk. She was Sisyphus, or some other Greek sad-sack, being punished for a crime she didn't remember committing. She was the butt of a joke. She glanced across the street to Prince's. This wasn't a coincidence. There was no way it was an accident. Someone—she was pretty sure she knew who—had put one of the most valuable Stashes inside her parents' store. This had been done on purpose. This was done to rub it in—sending people into the store all day long with no intention of buying anything. A deep hatred filled her blood. It pumped through her veins. This feeling, this was how one stupid feud could last for five decades.

She plopped down on the stool behind the counter and searched for the app on her phone. There it was, ready to be downloaded. What if she just joined, started playing the game like everyone else? It was stupid for her to be sitting here, right next to one of the more valuable Stashes, letting everyone pass her by. She could actually win this thing. She could get the plane tickets. If she coupled those with the money she was making from tutoring, she might actually be able to go on spring break with Harper this year.

And, on top of all that, it'd be sweet, sweet vengeance if she, a Chestnut, were the one to win a contest sponsored by Prince's Sporting Goods. Trip and Oliver would crap themselves.

Without a moment's hesitation, she downloaded the game and created a profile for herself. She was now "proud_hoser," her avatar looked like Harper, and she was down at the bottom of the leader board with a whopping zero points.

But not for long. She clicked on the name at the top of the list—StashIsMyCopilot—and composed a message, a heckle. "You're going down, my friend. You have no idea."

. . .

Oliver lay on his bed and held an index card up to the ceiling. "Tarquinius Superbus. His name means Tarquin the Proud. He tossed his father-in-law, King Servius Tullius, down the steps of the senate-house. His wife, Tullia, drove over her father's body with her carriage."

He turned the card over and read the rest of the information. Then he held the card to his forehead, like he was trying to learn the facts by osmosis. "And he refused to bury his father-in-law. His son assaulted a woman, causing an uprising and the end of the monarchy. That was in 509 BC, which marked the start of the Roman republic."

There was a knock on his door. "Come in!" he said.

Regina entered and perched on Oliver's desk chair. The desk itself was almost empty now, since his parents had taken away his computer, laptop, and tablet. His phone was his only connection to the outside world. And even if he'd wanted to use that to make changes on the Stash Grab game, he couldn't. His dad and sister had changed all the passwords. He was a prisoner in his own house.

"What do you want?" He flicked his notecards to the ground.

"Just checking up on you, seeing how you're doing?"

"I'm fine." He rolled over and faced the wall where he'd hung a poster of Wizard War, which he also wasn't allowed to play right now. His entire universe was taunting him. "No thanks to you."

"I'm the one who's trying to keep your game afloat. Some gratitude would be appreciated."

He sighed, focusing on the young wizard in the corner of his poster. That guy was having a better day than Oliver, and he was about to have his head blasted off by a spell.

"Anyway," Regina said. "'How are you, Regina? What's going on in your life?'"

"How are you, Regina? What's going on in your life?" Oliver muttered.

"I'm in a bit of a romantic pickle."

Oliver groaned. Regina was always using him as a

sounding board for her relationship problems. She never expected him to give her advice or anything—not that he'd even be able to give many words of wisdom. He wasn't very experienced at the whole dating game. He just got the impression that Regina liked talking to him mostly because he was a warm body in the room, like she believed it'd look weird if she hashed this stuff out on her own. "What kind of romantic pickle?" he asked.

"Well, I hooked up with someone on the ski trip."

"Fine, I'll play along," Oliver said. "Who did you hook up with?"

"Harper."

"So, you're dating Harper." This wasn't a total shock to Oliver. His sister had been out to him as bi for a long time now. He'd heard all about her various romances in Florida, and now Minnesota. She was good at falling in love, and out of it. She and Oliver were complete opposites that way. Every person Regina came into contact with was a potential story, a potential adventure. Everyone Oliver met…usually wanted to hang out with Regina instead.

"No, I'm not dating Harper," she said. "That's the problem. I was in kind of a bad place on the ski trip. I don't know if you noticed."

"I did not." Oliver only recalled seeing his sister running through the lodge lobby laughing and chatting while he was working away on the Stash Grab app.

"Well, I was. I told somebody right before break that I liked him, and he said he wasn't interested. So when Harper kind of made a move on the ski trip, I went along with it because I was sad and we were on vacation…"

Oliver flipped over so he could see his sister. Her knees sandwiched her hands. She reminded him of a dog with his tail between his legs. "Harper's your friend."

"Yeah." Regina frowned.

"You hooked up with your friend. That's never a good thing. I know virtually nothing about relationships—friendships or otherwise—and even I know that."

She frowned and scrunched up her face. "Believe me. I know it was stupid. I knew it was stupid before it happened."

"You didn't talk to her beforehand? You didn't hash this out?"

She shook her head. "It just kind of happened. I figured—I hoped—we were on the same page, but..." She groaned. "So, so stupid."

"Have you told her you just want to be friends?" Oliver's romantic experience was so limited, he wasn't sure if any of the advice he'd give would be the right advice. But, hey, he was trying.

Regina winced and shook her head.

"Regina."

"I know. It's just, Harper's really cool and I do like hanging out—as *friends*. I want to stay friends, and I don't want to hurt her feelings. It's a total 'it's not you, it's me' situation. The guy I liked, well, right after break he came here and said he couldn't stop thinking about me while I was gone. Ever since then, we've been seeing each other." She grinned like she couldn't stop herself.

"Who?" Oliver asked.

"It's new and fragile. I don't want to talk about it. Let me have my secrets, Ollie."

"Don't worry. I'll still be here in five minutes when you want to tell me all about this relationship, too." He sat up. "And, besides, it's Stan Stashiuk, isn't it?"

"That obvious?" She beamed.

"You need to talk to Harper."

"I was afraid that's what you'd say."

"That's literally what anyone would say, Regina. This is a no-brainer." He tapped his hands on his knees. "Sooooo..."

"I'm not talking to you about the game," she said.

"Come on. I talked to you about your love life."

"Barely."

"Fine." Shrugging, he stood up, picked up his index cards from the floor, and put them in his backpack. "Tell me, don't tell me, I don't care. This is a temporary situation."

"You're going to pass your Latin quiz?" she asked.

"I am," he said, Tarquinius Superbus facts running through his head. "I'm going to show Dad that I'm working hard and that I can balance everything. Then he'll give me the passwords and let me control the game again. Circle of life."

Regina shook her head.

Oliver shook his head back at her as his shoulders dropped. "What?"

"Just don't get your hopes up, Ollie."

"What? I pass my classes. I spend some time with the AV Club or whoever. I show some growth. I get my stuff back." That was the bargain. That was getting Oliver out of bed in the morning.

Regina cringed. "I said something to Dad about it, like maybe when Mom's gone, you can work on Stash Grab for at least an hour a day or something. He said no. Absolutely not. He doesn't want to piss Mom off." Her face got serious, even more serious. "I think there's something going on with them."

Oliver shrugged that off, avoiding the emotional conversation Regina was grasping for. Of course there was something going on with them. Anyone could see that. But what could he and Regina do about it? Their parents had been on the outs for years. "Now he decides to listen to Mom? Now?"

"Oliver, keep focus. What if they get divorced?"

"What if they do?" Oliver said. "What would change? Mom's already not here."

"What if she wants us to come back to Florida? I don't

want to go back."

Where was her concern a week ago? Two months ago? Two days ago, when he still had his computer? "Either way," he said. "At least in Florida we could be having this conversation by the beach."

Regina set her jaw and stood up. "You don't care about anyone, do you?"

"I'm a realist, Regina." He pointed to the door. "All of Mom and Dad's relationship stuff is out of our control. What can you or I even do about it?"

"You can talk to me. You can show some emotion about the situation and how it affects us." Her lip trembled. "You only care about yourself and your computers and your stupid game. I hope you never get any of them back."

She barged out and Oliver stood in the middle of his room, alone. Once the aftershock of the door slam subsided, he realized there was no sound in his room. He couldn't stand it. Usually there was some noise—the computer whirring, alerts chirping, keys clacking. Now there was nothing. He had nothing.

At least they'd left him his phone. He flopped onto the bed and pulled his phone out of his pocket. The hilarious thing was that his family wanted him to be more social, to talk to more people, but he'd never been spoken to more in his life than after the Stash Grab game started. He was suddenly Mr. Popular—*Oliver, where's this Stash? Oliver, how many Stashes are in the golf resort? Oliver, can you give me some answers?* His parents and Regina wanted him to hang out with people in real life, but all the real-life people were hanging out with his game. And he was stuck in this room by himself. It was stupid.

He went to the app store to download Stash Grab. What if he played? What if he joined the game? He could keep tabs on how Regina was doing that way. He could let his dad know when she screwed up. It'd be a way for him to at least do something, to be involved in some way.

He typed in a random, secret email address he used for spam to create his account, and then he called himself something so North Pole that no one would ever suspect it was him: Stashiuk4Prez. He fashioned his avatar after Bruce Wayne (the Christian Bale Bruce Wayne), because that's who Oliver was—the Batman of Stash Grab, lurking in the shadows to save the game.

He checked out the leader board to see how people were doing. Then a message popped up on his screen, a private message from some other player who wanted to chat. The person's name was proud_hoser. Her avatar was blond, compact, and muscular. He clicked on the conversation, expecting some kind of nice welcome or something.

Her message said, "Welcome to the party, pal. You're a little late."

"Hey, at least I showed up." He clicked on her profile. She wasn't too far ahead of him in the standings. "Big talk for someone about five slots above me on the leader board."

"Maybe I'm biding my time," she said.

"Until when? The game is over?"

She sent him back a crying-laughing emoji. "I like you. You're the first person to trash talk me back. The rest of this town is full of people who are way too polite for this nonsense."

"Politeness is overrated."

"Absolutely." Then she said, "Welcome to the game, Stashiuk4Prez. I look forward to kicking your ass."

Chapter Five

"Are you really a guy?" Elena asked. "Because I can't trust an avatar."

"I'm definitely a guy."

Elena grinned. She was leaning up against her locker, chatting with Stashiuk4Prez, something that had been happening a lot lately, though the two of them had mostly kept to Stash Grab basics—talking about North Pole and Stash trivia and pointing each other in the direction of various Stashes around town. They had only just started dipping their toes into sharing personal information—his problems with his sister, the annoying dude she "worked" with.

"What about you?" he asked. "Were you only asking if I'm a guy because you're not actually a girl?"

"No, I'm a girl," she said after a moment. These questions felt like big steps. They were crossing little Rubicons all over the place. "Should we discuss real names at this point?" she asked, flinching.

"I don't know," he said. "How about not yet? It's more fun this way, isn't it?"

"It is." She was half relieved. No one knew she was doing this competition, not Harper, not even her parents. She kind of just wanted to keep it to herself. If she succeeded and won the tickets, great. If not, no harm done, no egg on her face, no snide comments from Oliver Prince about her falling into the Stash Grab trap and having fun playing a stupid game he created.

"Just tell me one thing," she said. "For the love of God, please tell me you're not Craig."

"I'm not Craig."

"That feels like something Craig would say."

"I'm in high school," Stashiuk4Prez said.

Giddy, she hugged her phone. The guy she'd been chatting with was not an old man. Or Craig.

"I'm in high school, too," she said.

A hand slammed against the locker next to her. Elena shut off her phone's screen on reflex and peeked over at the perfectly manicured hand, though she'd have known who it was even if she hadn't spotted the bright pink nails. The spicy scent of Obsession was a dead giveaway. Harper.

"You were playing Stash Grab!" Harper said, reaching for the phone.

Elena shoved it behind her back. "No, I wasn't."

"Bullshit," said Harper, giving up on obtaining concrete evidence. "I saw you, and obviously I support this development. I want you to win those damn tickets for spring break."

"Don't tell anyone," said Elena.

"I won't."

"Especially not Oliver," Elena said. "I'd like to keep the upper hand there."

"Of course," Harper said.

The girls started walking toward the cafeteria for lunch. Elena kept her eyes peeled—but for what? Something, anything, the tiniest clue that might show her who

Stashiuk4Prez really was. What if he was doing the same thing right now? He was. He totally was. A new electricity pulsed through the air. Stashiuk4Prez was inside this building with Elena right now. He was here. He existed within these walls.

Elena hadn't felt these bubbly nerves in a while. She was developing a crush on someone she'd met online. She was that person now. She was the girl who liked the guy she'd only chatted with via text. And because she didn't know who Stashiuk4Prez was and therefore felt she could say anything to him, this down-low romance had hit her faster and fiercer than any other crush she'd ever had before.

Harper, too, was glancing around, searching for something or someone.

"How are things going with you two?" Elena asked. "You and Oliver?" She coughed out his name. They'd had a number of tutoring sessions over the past week, and while he'd made a concerted effort to learn his Latin facts, he continued acting like being in Elena's presence was some grave punishment. The feeling was mutual. And she really could not fathom what her best friend saw in him, beyond the hair and the eyes. And the sliver of lower back she'd seen peeking out from under his fleece when he bent over to grab a pen. Still, the rest of him was completely vile.

Harper stopped in her tracks and focused on Elena. "Nothing new with him."

Elena crinkled her nose. "I can...ask him about you, if you want. You know, when I'm tutoring him—"

Harper cut her off right away, waving her arms across her chest. "No, no, no. Don't do that. Definitely not."

"You're the boss." Elena patted her shoulder. "He's an idiot if he doesn't realize how great you are."

Harper rolled her eyes. "Thanks."

"Actually, having spent some quality time with him recently, I can tell you he's an idiot either way."

Later that afternoon, after Elena had devoted her final four periods to secretly hunting for Stashiuk4Prez in the halls and classrooms of North Pole High, her mom met her at the front door of their house and asked Elena to help deliver some golf clubs. Elena groaned. This was her one afternoon off—from either the store or Oliver Prince. She had hoped to sneak off on a long run to hunt Stashes around town, but alas. That was a no-go.

"Maggie Garland bought a set for her dad's birthday and they were accidentally delivered here," her mom said, handing a bulky blue golf bag to Elena. "He's staying at their house this week, and I told her I'd walk them over to the store so she could hide them from him."

The bottom of the golf bag thumped against the back of her leg as Elena trekked down Main Street, and her phone sat heavy inside her jeans pocket. She was itching to check it. All around her, people were staring at their phones, hunting for Stashes, bumping into lampposts and doors. She saw Craig and Dinesh racing—coatless, mittenless, and hatless—down the middle of the street.

Elena's mom shook her head, the box of golf balls and tees jiggling in her hands. "This game is going to kill someone, and all to get people to buy more skis. Trip Prince, always concerned about his bottom line."

"You know him?" asked Elena.

"A little," said her mom.

"The game is safe, Mom," said Elena.

"It is not." Her mom pointed to Craig, who had crashed smack-dab into the back of a parked car. "Look at this fool." Mrs. Chestnut glanced over at her daughter. "I'm just glad you have the good sense not to involve yourself in this idiocy. Keep yourself far away from the Princes' web of nonsense."

"Just like you taught me," said Elena, who was currently sitting pretty in the top ten on the leader board, thanks to a deep knowledge of Stan Stashiuk and banal North Pole trivia.

At the coffee house, Maggie Garland's two sons worked the counter while scanning their phones for Stashes. Brian, the older one, was a senior at North Pole High, but Danny was in Elena's class. He was super popular, the star of the basketball team. Danny won every contest he entered and was known for being super competitive—the kind of guy who would totally trash talk a girl back. Could he be Stashiuk4Prez? This was the conversation she'd been having with herself all day, about every guy she saw at school. But Danny had been dating Star since sophomore year…

Knitting his brow, Danny glanced up from his phone. "Can I help you?" He wiped his cheek like he was sure Elena had been staring at something on his face.

Elena shook her head, annoyed that she'd been caught watching him. She had to stop treating every guy like he might be Stashiuk4Prez.

Maggie, exiting the back room where she'd dropped off the golf clubs, came out and said, "Let me get you some coffee."

Elena gave her mom the side eye, not sure of the protocol here. Fancy, expensive espresso drinks were not within their budget. Elena knew that much.

"On the house," Maggie said after a moment. "Of course."

"Oh, oh," said Mrs. Chestnut. "Then okay. I'll just have a black coffee."

"Elena?" Maggie was smiling right at her.

"Vanilla latte with whipped—"

Mrs. Chestnut stepped on Elena's foot, hard. The pain made it through her boot and deep into her toes.

"I mean," Elena said, hopping slightly, "black coffee."

"Vanilla latte it is," Maggie said.

A buzzing from her phone tickled Elena's hip, and she made a move to grab it from her pocket, but then she caught sight of her mom standing right next to her. Elena's body tensed as she watched Danny and Brian spinning around, searching for the Stash. She longed to join them.

"This stupid game." Maggie, making the latte behind the counter, shook her head.

"I don't know how they haven't all been hit by cars," Mrs. Chestnut said. "At least Elena has the sense to sit this one out."

"You're not playing?" Maggie glanced up at Elena.

Elena shrugged. It was a non-answer answer.

"Good for you."

"Over here!" Brian shouted.

Elena spun around and watched as Brian and Danny, along with two other Santabucks patrons—older Joyces in their Christmas sweaters—hurried to the back corner of the cafe, right outside the ladies' room.

"'What was Stash's favorite subject in high school?'" Danny read out loud. "Hell if I know."

Elena's jaw tensed. She knew this one. It had been on this silly card Chestnut's had printed up when Stan Stashiuk was a rookie, like a baseball card, but for hockey and with a lot more personal information. His favorite subject was biology. She considered sneaking into the bathroom for a second to answer it.

"Gym?" Brian guessed.

"Biology," Elena blurted. She clamped her hand over her mouth.

Danny, Brian, and the other players spun toward her in unison, completely shocked.

"How did you know that?" Danny frowned. "No one knows that."

Elena shrugged. "Just do. I don't know."

Maggie grabbed Elena's mom's arm and pulled her toward the back room. "Let me show you the new cups I bought for Valentine's Day."

Her mom safely behind a closed door, Elena snuck over to a table with her latte and pulled out her phone. The Santabucks Stash had disappeared for now, but Elena started clicking on the little blue bubbles floating around her name on the main screen. She pressed one. It opened up and gave the info of another player in her vicinity. It had the person's name, score, and a button to start chatting.

She hit the other three bubbles. None of them was Stashiuk4Prez, which meant Danny wasn't Stashiuk4Prez, not that she really ever believed he was. Stashiuk4Prez would've told her he had a girlfriend—at least she hoped that'd be the case. The guy in her mind wouldn't string anyone along.

"Glad to see you're all enjoying the game."

Elena's eyes swung toward the door, and she found Mr. Prince standing there with his chest puffed out and shoulders back, watching the crowd, smiling. He towered above all of them like a king in his castle. His smile diminished, however, when his eyes landed on Elena. It got even smaller still, regressing to a full-on frown, when his gaze reached Elena's mom, who was stepping out of the back room just behind Maggie Garland.

Mr. Prince nodded slightly toward her, his eyes on the floor. "Emily."

"Nice to see you, Trip." Elena's mom's voice was steely, and she eye-rolled hard at Maggie Garland, who nodded.

"I bet." Mr. Prince stepped toward the counter, turning his back on Emily Chestnut.

Elena shoved her phone in her pocket as her mom gestured frantically toward the door. They hurried out of the store and down the street toward Chestnut's, their coffees sloshing over their mittened hands.

"What was all that about?" Elena asked, when they reached the door to their own store.

"Ancient history," her mom said, discussion over. She glanced one more time down the street toward Santabucks, pulled open the door to Chestnut's, and slid inside with a huff.

Elena stared down the street at the cafe. From where she stood, that history didn't look so ancient.

• • •

Trip Prince had made sure that Oliver and Regina knew how to do every job in each of the many shops the family had owned. "You can't understand the business side of things if you don't know how to deal with the day-to-day operations." So, Oliver knew how to make sandwiches, bake a pizza in a brick oven, and sell a pair of skis, even though he had no idea how to use those skis himself.

Today was his day to stock shelves and take inventory inside Prince's Sporting Goods. He was on the floor in the summer clearance aisle when the front doorbell rang. Their new employee, Craig, who was manning the cash register, said, "Good afternoon. May I help you?"

"Help me? This is my store," Regina said, followed by a massive giggle that hadn't come from his sister's mouth.

Oliver peeked around the corner and saw Regina standing at the counter, checking her phone. Harper was right next to her. She only came up to Regina's shoulder, and she was bouncing on her tiptoes either to get Regina's attention or to peek at her phone. Regina turned away, hiding the screen with her body.

Shoulders slumped, Harper scanned the rest of the store.

Oliver ducked back behind the shelves and tried to make himself small, crouching near the ground. Maybe Harper hadn't seen him yet. Maybe he could slither across the floor and sneak into the office undetected.

"I'm going into the back for a minute," said Regina.

Oliver swore under his breath when he heard the office door slam shut. Regina was always quick to leave him alone with Harper, as if she expected Oliver to do her dirty work and break the bad news. Regina was still trying to figure out a way to let Harper down easy.

Oliver could feel Harper's presence in the room, her aura. He could sense her sweeping the area. She was going to find him, and then she'd bombard him with questions about his sister. The kind thing would be to set Harper straight, to tell her that Regina wasn't interested and that she never would be, but he couldn't do it. Why should he have to be the bad guy? This was Regina's situation, and she should get herself out of it. Just because Oliver didn't do well in relationships with other people didn't mean he was cool with destroying the tenuous ones he had.

He heard Harper ask Craig, "Is Oliver here?"

Oliver sent a silent message to Craig's brainwaves, pleading with him to tell Harper he'd gone home for the day.

"Sale section," said Craig, that traitor.

Harper's heels clomped toward Oliver. There was no way out of this. She was going to engage him in yet another Regina-centric conversation. Yet again, he'd have to come up with excuses for his sister's poor behavior.

"Hey, Oliver," Harper said, leaning up against the shelves. She was wearing a tight sweater and a short skirt, basically her uniform.

"Hi, Harper," he said casually. "What's going on?"

"Not much." She absentmindedly twirled a strand of her long, blond hair around a perfectly manicured finger while staring wistfully at the office door. "You need any help?"

He stood up, wiping his hands on his jeans. "I'm about done." He examined Harper's profile. She was still watching the office door, behind which Regina had disappeared. Oliver's first impulse was to run, to let the girls handle their own drama; but, going completely against his nature, he gulped, leaned toward Harper, and whispered, "Are you okay?"

Her face swung to his, eyes shocked. Oliver figured she was going to tell him off, to mind his own business, but she didn't. Her face softened and she said, "I will be. Thanks for asking."

Oliver grinned, and he noticed his body felt lighter. He couldn't believe he was about to say this, but, "If you ever need anyone—"

"Hey Harper," shouted Regina from the front of the store. "Ready to go?"

Harper leaned in and patted his arm. He got a whiff of her perfume—spicy and mature, not at all like the kind of perfume he'd expect Harper to choose. She whispered to Oliver, "I think you're a good guy, no matter what Elena says."

As the girls left, he moved to the next aisle—fishing supplies. Beaming like a goofball, he leaned against the shelf and pulled out his phone to open the Stash Grab app. He clicked on his conversation with proud_hoser, which was a thing he did reflexively now. It was second nature. Open app, chat with proud_hoser. "I just found out I'm a good guy," he said. "Got the info from a reliable source, and I wanted you to know. I have bonafides."

He started counting lures while waiting for her to respond. He was used to chatting with people online, via Wizard War and his other games, but talking to proud_hoser was different. Their relationship had started out as trash talk, but it had quickly evolved into something he'd never experienced before. She wasn't just a competitor and sometime co-conspirator. She was proud_hoser, a girl he thought about constantly, and he really, really desperately needed her to know he was a decent person.

A few minutes later, she wrote back, "Glad to hear it. I

always trust anonymous sources." Then she said, "How's your afternoon?"

Oliver was currently surrounded by boxes, the smell of stale coffee, and Craig, who kept making some unsettling hacking sound up front. "Low-key," he said. "Kind of boring. How about you?"

"Getting better," she said. "I'm about to go for a run."

"You're a runner," he said. "A clue!"

"Just one of millions who do it. Do you run?"

Oliver laughed. "I'm not a sports guy."

"There's my clue!"

"Are you running outside? It's like three degrees out." The Florida boy in him couldn't spend more than five minutes outside in this January-in-Minnesota weather.

"It clears my head. You should try it. Smacks the life right into you."

"Maybe someday," he lied. Though, a part of him wondered if he wouldn't like running better if he had a partner—someone exactly like proud_hoser, perhaps. Oliver caught himself blushing. What was he doing? Was he actually imagining they could take this relationship offline? Danger, Will Robinson! Oliver wasn't an offline guy. "What needs clearing?"

"Huh?" she asked.

"From your head." For the second time today, Oliver was sticking his nose into other people's business. It shocked him to discover that he really did want to know how proud_hoser was doing—and Harper, for that matter. He was going soft without his video games.

"It's dumb," she said.

"Try me."

Oliver waited as she typed a longer response. He straightened the fishing poles and tackle boxes. Each second was an hour. He jumped when his phone pinged with a new message.

"Remember you're the one who asked. I was thinking about how we only show other people a carefully curated version of ourselves."

Oliver exhaled. That was unexpected. Oliver had imagined she'd tell him something like, "I don't like chicken soup" or "I think we should stop chatting, Stashiuk4Prez. I know who you are and you're an awful, boring person."

"Deep stuff for a Wednesday afternoon," he replied.

"I have a lot on my mind at the moment."

Oliver considered Regina, the person he knew best on the entire planet. Regina always seemed so cool and confident, but deep down she cared more about being popular than she'd ever let on. She and Oliver were really two sides of the same coin—she was afraid of losing the popularity she'd always had, and he was afraid of being rejected by the same crowd, so he never sought out the popularity. "I definitely put up a wall in real life. I act like I don't need anyone else and that I'm kind of bored with all the social garbage, but maybe I'm afraid of being told I don't belong, you know? Ha-ha, that's for sure the most honest I've ever been with anyone, and you're just a tiny avatar on my phone."

"I guess it's easier to be honest with an avatar."

Yes, it was so much easier to be honest with a non-corporeal image than a real, living person. Oliver could carefully select every word, delete the ones that came out wrong, and answer in his own time. There was no fretting about coming off cold and callous or accidentally turning someone off because of "tone."

"What has you wondering about all this?" he asked.

"Ah, my mom. She said something that got me thinking about how she had this whole life before I was born. My dad, too. What were they like? What were their dreams? Did they always know they'd end up together? That kind of thing."

She had parents. She had parents and she ran and she knew more about Stan Stashiuk than any high school girl should. proud_hoser was taking shape in his mind's eye, and he ate up every morsel of information like his grandma's famous pumpkin pie. "I never really thought about all that, but you're right," Oliver said. "They were young once. I suppose."

proud_hoser wrote, "Did they have secret, anonymous chats about life with strange boys in high school? :)"

He blushed. "I don't know, but—"

"Oliver!" shouted Craig from the front of the store. "I need your help!"

"Damn it," Oliver said. He wrote, "I'm sorry, but I have to go."

"Me, too," she said, "I've got to get that run in. Talk tonight?"

"Definitely." Always. Whenever she wanted.

"And I promise to keep the conversation lighter. We can talk favorite movies and TV shows."

He couldn't end the chat. He was physically unable to do so. Forget Craig. Forget work. "*Captain America: Winter Soldier* and *The Simpsons*," he said right away.

"Oliver!" shouted Craig again.

"Save it for later," said proud_hoser.

Oliver went up to the front of the store. Craig was standing alone in front of a display of snowboards. "What's happening, Craig?"

"There's a glitch," he said.

"A glitch?"

Craig held up his phone. The Stash Grab app was open. "When you click on this Stash, nothing happens. Watch." Craig clicked on the Stash. He was right. Nothing happened.

Oliver opened up his own app.

"You're playing, too?" Craig asked, craning his head to see Oliver's phone. "Isn't that cheating? You created the game." Craig's eyes scanned the room, like he was about to pull an alarm somewhere, if only he could find it.

Oliver hid the screen. "I have a dummy account," he said. "For just this kind of thing."

He found the Stash in Prince's and tried to click it. Nothing happened. "Damn it." He closed the app, fiddled with the settings, and tried again. Still nothing.

"Can you fix it?" asked Craig. "It's worth three hundred points."

"I can't." He glanced at the office. Maybe he could hack into the computer. Maybe it was worth a try. This kind of glitch was unacceptable. What was Regina doing with her time?

Oliver marched into the office and shut the door behind him. He sat in front of the computer and cracked his knuckles. A wave of emotion hit him. "Hi, old friend." He rubbed the cover of the laptop, like he was petting a dog, before opening it.

He pressed a key and the screen whirred to life. A login box popped up, asking for his username and password. He tried one he knew Regina had used before—nothing. He tried his dad's email address and another old password, still nothing. They had really done their due diligence. His dad did not want him to get on this computer.

But they weren't that smart. They wouldn't have created these new logins without leaving the information somewhere. He opened the desk drawers, one by one, searching for some clue that would give him access to this computer.

What he found instead, in the bottom drawer, was the old photo album Regina had found a few weeks ago, the book that had sent his dad running into the office and slamming the door behind him. Gingerly, like it was a bomb he had to diffuse, Oliver lifted the book from the drawer. He placed it on the desk in front of him and slowly opened it, bracing himself for whatever lurked inside.

His heart slowed as he surveyed the first pictures. They were just family photos of his grandparents with his dad and Aunt Becky. There were shots of the store and of his dad playing basketball for North Pole High. Then there was a page near the back that made him pause. It was his dad, but he was much younger. He had a full head of auburn hair (like Oliver's) and no beard. He had his arm around some woman—not his mom—and the two of them were gazing into each other's eyes.

The woman gave him a sense of déjà vu, like he'd seen her before, but couldn't figure out when. She had a very familiar look about her. Then he knocked the album to the ground as he realized why. She was the spitting image of Elena Chestnut.

His dad had his arm wrapped around Elena's mom. Was this what Regina had seen? Did she know any more about it? Did Elena?

Slowly, still trying to figure this out, Oliver reached down, closed the book, and placed it back into the drawer. He now understood completely what proud_hoser had been talking about. What did he truly know about anybody, especially his dad?

Chapter Six

Elena checked her skirt in Harper's bedroom mirror after dropping her parka on the bed, which was already a sea of other people's coats. She smoothed down a wrinkle, then frowned and dropped her shoulders.

"Hey, Elena," said Katie Murphy, depositing her coat at the summit of the outerwear mountain on Harper's bed. "Haven't seen you out in a while."

"I think I've been hibernating," said Elena.

Katie checked her lip gloss. "I feel you. January."

Elena waved to Katie as she left the room. The fact was, if this weren't a birthday party for her best friend, Elena wouldn't have come to this party, either.

She grabbed her purse and a special gift for the always fashion-forward Harper—an amazing vintage capelet Elena had found at a thrift store—and headed out to join the rest of Harper's guests.

Harper was incapable of throwing a small to-do. Whenever she threw a party, it had to be a blowout, a huge bash. There were balloons and streamers in Harper's favorite colors—

blush and bashful, like from the movie *Steel Magnolias*, also one of Harper's favorites—covering every bare inch of wall space. She'd put together little pink gift bags with *macarons* from Joyeaux Noel, the fancy French restaurant in town and lip glosses. The entire house was crawling with students from North Pole High School, who were shouting at each other over the aggressive *thump-thump* of Craig's DJ booth.

As she placed her tiny gift on the overflowing table of presents, Elena checked the clock on the wall to figure out how long she'd have to stick around before making a clean exit.

Her first order of business was getting Harper to notice she was here. Elena pushed her way through the crowd—bumping into dancers, knocking into their drinks and plates of appetizers. Despite the cold, most of the girls had stripped out of their winter gear and into short skirts and tank tops. It was a party, after all.

Elena finally spotted Harper down in the basement on the sectional couch, sitting right next to—practically on top of—Oliver Prince. Despite the noise, they both looked up when Elena reached the bottom stair. Harper frantically waved Elena over, but Elena pointed to the soda bar at the other end of the room. She was not going to spend the evening talking to Oliver Prince. Not when she wasn't getting paid for it.

The Andersons always stocked the best pop in their house—rare kinds their dad found when he was traveling for work, expensive small batch sodas, even the really basic generic cream soda Harper liked from the grocery store. The house was totally dry. No one from school would dare to complain about the lack of alcohol at Harper's parties. Her mom was killed by a drunk driver—some tourist—back in junior high, only about a year after the Andersons had moved to town. It was during the summer, on a two-lane road just south of town that was always slick when it rained.

After the funeral, Harper's dad had gotten rid of every drop of alcohol in the house on principle. Elena had sat on the couch between Harper and her brother, Sam, gripping Harper's hand, and watched it all happen.

Harper's situation reminded Elena of what she'd talked to Stashiuk4Prez about the other night. Anyone who'd just met Harper would have no idea the tragedy her family had faced. She always put on a strong front. It was only when you got to know her that she'd let you see her emotions.

Elena, however, knew the real Harper. They'd been through a lot together—her mom's death, and Elena's grandmother's. They'd cried when Star and some of the other girls had bullied Elena in eighth grade. They'd laughed and swooned over the romantic comedies they both loved—*While You Were Sleeping* and *How to Lose a Guy in 10 Days*. They fed each other gooey nachos and under-baked chocolate chip cookies. Only Harper knew that Elena's anxious mind woke her up at two o'clock every morning, and she watched old sitcoms until she fell back asleep. Only Elena knew that Harper wore Obsession perfume because it was her mom's scent, or that she slept with a ratty old doll every night because she was scared of the dark.

But now Harper was hiding something about the Christmas ski trip with Oliver Prince, Elena wasn't telling Harper about the troubles at her family's store, and she hadn't mentioned her chat relationship with Stashiuk4Prez. Why?

They had been knocked out of synch, and there was a pretty obvious reason why—it all started and ended with the Prince family.

After grabbing a bottle of her favorite pop (Coca-Cola from Mexico, made with real sugar, not gross corn syrup), Elena ducked upstairs to the front room, which was empty, perched in the dark on one of the wing-backed armchairs, and opened her Stash Grab app.

The thumping bass and loud conversations faded into background noise as she clicked on every blue bubble, hunting for one specific name. None of them belonged to Stashiuk4Prez. Either he wasn't here tonight or he didn't have his app open. Whatever the reason, it sunk her heart.

Defeated, she dragged herself into the family room off the back of the house where she found Sam Anderson talking to Danny, Star, and Marley. Sam waved when Elena entered the room, and she settled into an empty spot on the couch across from him. At least there were no Princes in this room. At least she was safe here.

"Elena knows what I'm talking about," he said, gesturing toward her. "Harper is a huge slob."

She held up her pop bottle in a salute of agreement.

Sam winked at Elena, then addressed his audience. "So, yeah. I couldn't find my phone anywhere in her room, it's such a disaster area. And I was like, 'Harper, can you please get in here and move your underwear? I've got Stashes to catch.'"

"Did you find it?" asked Marley, leaning forward.

"Finally." He reached into the pocket of his athletic shorts—Sam always wore athletic shorts, no matter the temperature—and held up his phone. "I hadn't even left it in her room. It was in the kitchen freezer." He rolled his eyes. "I had to wait, like, an hour for the thing to thaw out."

Danny took a sip of his pop, some fancy root beer with an ironic name. "Dude, don't make excuses."

"Excuses for what?" asked Sam.

Danny grinned. "Excuses for why you're losing so bad at Stash Grab."

Sam threw a pillow at him. "I'm not losing that bad." He rested his arms behind his head. "It's a fun game, though, isn't it? Like, the game itself is great, but it's also cool talking to people anonymously who could be your neighbor or your teacher or, hell, Craig, but you have no idea. It's amazing. Like in the movies. I started trash talking with some girl—"

When he said it, Elena was right in the middle of a huge gulp of pop. It went straight up her nose and sent her into a wild coughing, sneezing fit. Did he—her best friend's brother, a student at North Pole High—just say that he he'd been trash talking with some girl? Was it possible? It couldn't be possible.

Before he could finish his story, Sam jumped up and helped Elena to her feet. "You okay?" he asked, patting her on the back.

She pulled away from him slightly, off balance and confused and unsure of how to feel in this moment. Sam was chatting with some girl. Stashiuk4Prez was chatting with some girl. Was it just a coincidence? Obviously, she and Stashiuk4Prez couldn't have been the only two contestants who'd struck up a conversation over the past few weeks.

Elena gazed into Sam's big brown eyes. He brushed a curly lock of brown hair out of his face and smiled down at her. Though he always wore his omnipresent faded T-shirts and mesh basketball shorts, they worked on him. Sam was Sam. He was effortless, funny, and sweet. And he was always very nice to her. What if he were Stashiuk4Prez? Would that be so bad? Elena smiled up at him. "I'm okay," she said with what she hoped was a hint of meaning behind it.

"Good," Sam said, unceremoniously letting her go and flopping back down on the couch, his story abandoned. He launched into more trash talk with Danny. "At least I don't need my girlfriend to answer questions for me."

"Because, dude," said Danny, "you don't have a girlfriend."

Elena resumed her place on the couch, but kept watching Sam, observing him in a new light. She tried to imagine herself with Sam—hugging him, kissing him. It felt weird, and not, like, sexy, tingly weird. It felt brother-and-sister weird. But maybe that was because she'd never given the idea any consideration before. He'd always just been Sam, her friend's older brother. She'd never considered him to be Sam, boyfriend material. She stared at his lips. They were plump and supple, like they'd be fine to kiss. Elena caught herself licking her own lips, and nearly bit her tongue off when someone plopped down on the couch next to her.

Wincing in pain, she turned and met the deep, brown eyes of that trash heap in human form, Oliver Prince.

"What do you want?" What was Oliver doing staring at her like that? It was rude. She hadn't had to tutor him in three days and her life had never been better—no stubborn quips about the uselessness of learning a dead language (even though, hello, she'd helped him score a 96 percent on his Roman kings quiz), no yelling, no awkward silences.

"Can I talk to you a minute?" He nodded toward the other room. "Please," he said. "One minute."

"No," she said, focusing on Sam again.

"Please," he repeated.

She turned toward him. Oliver was frowning at her like he was about to deliver some life-altering, terrible news, like he was a doctor who knew Elena had three months to live. She didn't want to hear whatever this was, but she knew she had to listen. "Okay," she said. "But only because you said please. I want to encourage the modicum of polite behavior you've exhibited tonight."

Sneaking one last peek at Sam's mouth, which was now taunting Danny about his jump shot, Elena heaved herself off the overstuffed couch and followed Oliver into the dark dining room. He flipped on the lights, which sent star forward, Kevin Snow, and his flavor of the week, Katie Murphy this time, scrambling out of the room, fiddling with their clothes, making sure all their bits were covered. Elena groaned. She knew that life. She'd been Kevin's flavor of the week once. She shuddered. What if he were Stashiuk4Prez? That would be…not ideal.

Elena folded her arms and focused on Oliver. "Your minute starts now."

Oliver ran his fingers through his stupid-gorgeous russet hair. He didn't deserve that hair. He waited until the two of them were for sure alone, then he said, leaning toward her slightly, his voice softer than she was used to, "Do you… happen to know why our parents hate each other?"

"Uh, duh." She shrugged. What the hell? This was why he'd pulled her away? So she could stand here and listen to this foolishness instead of gathering clues about whether or not Sam and Stashiuk4Prez were the same person? "The feud," Elena said. "Obviously. Your grandfather bilked my grandfather out of, like, a year's worth of profits."

"That's not the way I heard, it," he said, narrowing his eyes, "but whatever. Is that the extent of it?"

She shrugged again, shaking her head, thinking about her mom's reaction to Trip Prince in Santabucks. Her eyes had haunted Elena for days. "Yeah, that's it. What else would it be?"

There were heavy, clomping footsteps behind them, and Oliver ducked down, using Elena's body to shield him from the door. She spun around to see what all the noise was about and saw Harper's diaphanous blue skirt trailing past the doorway.

"You'd better be nice to her," Elena said.

"I am nice to her." Oliver frowned, but he didn't move. He kept using Elena's body as a barrier between himself and Harper in the kitchen.

"You're using me as a human shield," Elena said.

Oliver peered over Elena's shoulder into the kitchen. "Because the last thing I want is anyone to see me talking to you when I'm not being forced to do so."

"You're the one who dragged me in here." He was still

watching the kitchen, making sure they were alone. "What happened between you two?" Elena bit her cheek and tapped her toe on the floor. If this guy hurt Harper…

"Between me and Harper? Nothing." Oliver's eyes snapped to Elena's.

"Nothing?" Elena said. "She's been acting weird ever since the trip over Christmas break. I've never seen her go gaga over anyone like she's gone over you."

He snorted. The corner of each eye crinkled in an annoyingly adorable way. She pinched her arm. *Stop thinking those things.*

"What?" Elena asked, focusing on his chin in order to avoid those eyes.

"Well, it's not me she's gaga over, is it?" He kept smiling at Elena like the two of them were in on this big secret together.

"What?" Elena said. "What are you even talking about?"

Oliver stared at her. "The trip…the hookup."

"Yeah," Elena said. "She hooked up with you."

Oliver's mouth dropped open.

"Right?" Elena asked, her heart speeding up.

Oliver didn't say anything.

"Right?" A flush crept up her neck. She knew Harper had been hiding something from her, but what was it? And why?

"I think you need to talk to your friend." Oliver frowned. "It's not my place to say anything."

"What is she not telling me?"

"Again." Oliver nodded toward the door to the kitchen. "Talk to her."

"I'll do that, person who just moved here and has no idea about anything." God, these Princes were such know-it-alls, so full of themselves. First his dad had traipsed into town and ruined her family's business, now Oliver was telling Elena that he knew more about her own best friend than she did. Elena spun on her heel and stepped toward the door.

But Oliver reached for her arm before she could get very far. Elena brushed him away immediately, though her skin tingled from his touch. He backed away, hands raised, like he hadn't meant to do that.

"What. The. Hell?" she asked, staring pointedly at his rogue hand.

"I found a picture, in Prince's," he whispered from halfway across the room. "Of your mom and my dad. That's what I wanted to tell you. They had their arms around each other, like they knew each other...well."

Ice spread through her body as she clutched the spot on her arm where Oliver's fingers had just grazed her. "What?" Elena asked.

Like tossing a Frisbee, he flung her the photograph, which fluttered to the floor between them. Elena picked it up. There they were, his dad and her mom, but twenty years younger, with their arms around each other. Elena blinked a few times, taking it all in, her heart pounding. "Whatever," she said. "So what?"

"So what?" he asked. "Your mom is staring at my dad like she adores him."

"No," said Elena, tossing the photo onto the dining room table. She wasn't going to make a fool of herself hurling it back at him. "Your dad has his arm around her shoulders and she's obviously sending out an SOS with her eyes." Oliver was right. This meant something. Elena had heard for years about the Princes and their vindictiveness, but she'd always understood the feud to be business-related. Her mom ogling Trip Prince like she wanted to lick him was not business. But Elena was not about to discuss it with Oliver freaking Prince.

"What do you think—?" Oliver started to say, as he put the picture back in his pocket.

But Elena's phone buzzed and her hand instinctively went to her purse. Behind her, in the kitchen, more phones buzzed and pinged. "I guess there's a Stash here." She shrugged, dropping her arms to her sides. She itched to take out her phone, to go after the Stash, but she knew she couldn't. Not in the presence of this doofus.

"You want to go get it?" asked Oliver.

Elena reeled back in feigned outrage. "I'm not playing that asinine game." She glanced at Oliver who was staring— What was it? Wistfully?—at the crowd of North Pole teenagers darting through the Anderson household. "Are we done here?"

"We're done."

"Good."

Clutching her purse to her side, she casually stepped into the kitchen, careful to avoid being stampeded by the entire varsity offensive line. People all around her dashed about, phones in the air. Sam and Danny were pulling their boots on, about to head outside. A crowd had already gathered in the yard. They trudged through the snow on the deck, tramped through the eight inches piled up in the grass, and skidded over Harper's little sister's makeshift ice rink as they ran toward the lake at the edge of the Andersons' property. Marley Ho fell face first into a drift, and Kevin Snow helped her up.

And Elena stood at the window and watched, because stupid Oliver Prince was right behind her and she didn't want to tip her hand.

"They're having fun," he said.

"Whatever." Elena folded her arms. She longed to be with them. A dull ache formed in her gut as she mentally popped bubbles in her head, wondering if any of them belonged to Stashiuk4Prez. But instead she was standing with her face pressed up against the glass, stuck in another inane conversation with her mortal enemy.

She turned slightly to face Oliver, to see what he was up

to. He had his phone in his hand, but the screen was black. "You have to be loving this."

He turned to her, brow furrowed.

"Everybody playing your game, having fun." She gestured toward the crowd gathering on the pier at the edge of the Andersons' property. "You did this."

He sighed. His eyes were focused on Danny's brother, Brian, as he frolicked across the snowdrifts in the yard of the abandoned house next door. "I can't really enjoy it, though, can I?"

"You still did it. Nobody'd be outside killing themselves right now if not for you." She watched Danny Garland crawl onto the ice next to the pier.

"There was a glitch," he said. "The Stash in Prince's wasn't working, and I couldn't get on the computer to fix it. I couldn't do anything about it. When I texted Regina to let her know, she was like, 'It's handled.' I'm worthless." Still staring outside, he bit his lip.

"You're not *worthless*," she said. "You're bringing your grades up and, you know, you'll get your computer back soon. And stuff."

"Yeah. Maybe." He turned to her, his eyes wide. "Thanks. For that."

"I heard," she said, clearing her throat and ending the moment of bizarre civility with Oliver Prince, "that your little game here has sparked some online romance."

Oliver's mouth dropped open. "I hadn't heard anything."

Elena said, "Sam said that he'd been chatting with some girl…"

Oliver laughed maniacally, relief painted on his face. "Is that what he said?"

"What's so funny? He met a girl through your game."

He paused his chortle long enough to tell her, "You didn't let him get to the punchline. He assumed he'd been chatting with a girl, but it turned out to be Mags from the diner." Oliver's eyes danced as he gazed down at Elena. She hated that he was laughing at her, like she was a fool or a child or something. She hated even more that he looked cute while doing it. "He did get some free burgers out of it."

"Oh." Elena watched Sam as he jumped up and down on the pier, nearly falling into the icy water, having answered the question right. In all likelihood, he wasn't Stashiuk4Prez. A sense of calm washed over her, relief, which startled her. Elena had been expecting sadness.

. . .

On Sunday, the day after her party, Harper showed up at the Princes' house right around lunch. Oliver, who was in the middle of doing homework after a grueling hour of tutoring with Elena at Santabucks, was the one who answered the door.

"Regina's not here," he said. She had been asleep when he left earlier that morning. He'd put a Post-It on her forehead, saying, "Nice Stash on the pier last night. Huge success."

"That's fine," Harper said. "What are you doing?"

Oliver cocked a wary eyebrow at her. "Homework?"

"Cool." Harper pushed her way in and headed straight to the kitchen.

Oliver, dumbstruck, followed her.

"I'm bored." She rummaged around in the Princes' cabinets and pulled out a pot, some oil, and a jar of popcorn. "Elena's working. Sam's working. Your sister's wherever." She held up a measuring cup. "This okay? I probably should've asked first."

Oliver shrugged. "I like popcorn."

She tossed three test kernels into the heating oil and put a lid on the pot. "You have fun at my party last night?"

"Yeah," he said, folding his arms and leaning against the counter. He wasn't sure what to do with himself. He wasn't sure what this was. Were he and Harper...hanging out? Spontaneous social situations were not Oliver's forte. He usually needed to prep himself for person-to-person interactions. But Harper had barged in out of nowhere, shaking up his day. He wracked his brain for a way to politely tell her to get the hell out. He had things to do. He had proud_hoser to chat with.

Harper turned to him. "Did you really have fun?"

"Sure." No, he hadn't. He'd spent the night stuck in a house full of people he didn't want to talk to, with people asking him questions about the game he'd created but was no longer in charge of. He'd longed to check his phone to see if proud_hoser was there, but he couldn't do it, not with so many other people around.

"Liar." Harper grinned, turning to check the heating kernels.

"Hey," he said, "I had the great misfortune of talking to Elena last night. Why haven't you told her about you and Regina?" Elena had tried drilling him again that morning about Harper's ski trip hook-up. He'd told her, "Let's stick to the Latin, please. It's what you're being paid for." Then she'd thrown an eraser at his face.

Exhaling, Harper turned and shook the pan. Oliver didn't know Harper very well, but he knew her type. Harper was a tough, strong, popular girl who always got her way. She was the queen bee. But standing in front of him right now, she was anything but. She was wounded. She looked all doe-eyed and pathetic, like Regina after a particularly bad breakup. They weren't so different, the two of them.

"Would Elena not understand?"

Harper turned around, surprised. "It's not that. Of course it's not that. It's just...I don't know what to tell her. I'm still trying to figure the whole thing out myself." Darkness crossed her face. "I've always gone out with guys and it was fine, but with Regina it just felt…right."

Oliver nodded slowly, scared of what he'd gotten himself into with this conversation. He wanted to be there for Harper, but he did not want the details of her romantic liaison with his sister. This situation right here was precisely why he'd spent most of his life avoiding emotional entanglements.

"My whole life," Harper continued, "I believed I was one thing, and now…I don't know. Am I gay? Am I bi? Is it just Regina?"

Ugh, just Regina. Another way he and his sister were polar opposites—she had some kind of magical powers that drew people to her, and Oliver was basically spray repellant for humans. The test kernels popped, and he nudged Harper out of the way. He poured a measuring cup full of popcorn into the pot and tossed the lid on top. "Regina is…" He struggled with how to finish that sentence.

"Special?" asked Harper.

"She's the heroine in her own romance series," he said, turning back to Harper. "She loves love. She's…kind of the anti-me." He laughed mirthlessly.

"You hate people and love?" Harper blinked.

"No. I don't know why I said that."

"Do you wish you were more like her?" she asked. "Also, I thought this was my therapy session. I'm the one trying to suss out her sexual identity."

"I'm sorry for hijacking the conversation," he said.

"I'm not," said Harper. "I came over here to get away from the swirling vortex inside my brain for a few minutes. Let's talk about your thing. Do you wish you were more like Regina?"

He shook the pot, just for something to do. The kernels were popping rapidly. "I don't want to be like her. Regina's life is exhausting—see this friend, text that one, meet here, go there. It's too much. I like peace. I like my computer."

"Which you don't have anymore," added Harper.

"A temporary setback." Soon he'd have his computer back, and everything would be normal.

Harper frowned. "I envy you," she said. "Sometimes I feel so needy, having to be around people all the time. I mean, I freaking showed up at your house this morning unannounced." She winced. "I'm sorry about that."

"It's okay," he said, shaking the pot again.

"Sometimes it's like, 'Harper, why can't you be by yourself for five minutes?'"

Oliver gave a mirthless smile to the popping corn.

"I'm afraid of being alone. It's what my brother Sam says. He's fine with being by himself—watching movies or whatever. I always get too in my head when left to my own devices. That's why I love having Elena around—when she is around. She hasn't been as much lately."

Oliver turned off the burner and listened as the popping subsided. "What's it like to have a person?"

"What do you mean?"

"You have Elena. You can count on her. I think about this a lot. If something terrible happened, if I found out I was sick or if someone broke my heart, I'd have no one to go to. There's no one I could call and know they'd have my back." He thought of proud_hoser. He'd tell her those things, but how pathetic was that? He only believed he could count on her because the two of them had never met face-to-face. "I have no one." He kept his eyes on the pot, which had long since stopped popping, because he couldn't look at Harper.

Harper padded up behind him, lifted up the lid, and grabbed a handful of popcorn. "Well, you're kind of a jerk."

"Thanks?" he said, watching her.

She shrugged, munching. "It's true, though. You're always

walking through the halls fast, like you have no time for anyone else. You're either on your phone or your computer or you're wearing earbuds. You give off this 'I don't give a fuck' aura. I—and probably everyone else—have always assumed you don't actually give a fuck."

He stared at the cabinet behind her head for a few beats. "I think I do give a fuck."

"Good." Harper grabbed another handful of popcorn. "Now you know, and knowing is half the battle." When she finished chewing, she put her hands on his shoulders. "Look, I'm sorry I said you're a jerk."

He pursed his lips.

"But obviously you're not a total jerk. You let your enemy's best friend and your sister's one-time hook-up make random popcorn in your kitchen, and you were totally cool about it."

He rolled his eyes. "Well, I'm a very cool guy."

"Here's the thing, Oliver: If you want to keep living your solitary computerized existence, fine. Keep doing that. You've got that locked down. But if you want people to want to hang out with you, you have to start letting them into your life. And that means dealing with the inconvenience of having social obligations."

He groaned.

"I know. But you can do this, if you want to. The first step is to stop acting like every interaction is a waste of your time."

"I don't."

"You do."

"It's not that I think I'm better than anyone," he said. "Just the opposite, actually. I know people think I'm weird or whatever, and I don't want to be rejected."

"Well, who does? Being rejected sucks. But it's the risk you have to take if you want to make friends."

Oliver munched on some popcorn. "I do want to make

friends."

"Good."

"How do I do that, though? Like, do I just go up to your brother and say, 'Hi, Sam. Be my friend.'"

"Well, I wouldn't say it like that, but you have all the tools. You're smart, you can be amusing, and, Oliver Prince, you're a beautiful, beautiful male-type person. You look like—who's the guy from the show? Ugh." She hit her head, wracking her brain. "I'm sure Sam would know, speaking of." She pulled out her phone and started texting. "But maybe you should start with not letting 'dick wad' be your default setting." She sent the text, then snapped her fingers. "Practice on Elena."

Oliver scrunched up his nose.

"I mean it. This is brilliant. I'm brilliant for coming up with this. If you can be nice to her, you can be nice to anyone."

He let out a deep, rumbling sigh, and was about to tell her why that was a terrible idea, when her phone buzzed. "Robb Stark! That's who you look like."

"It's just the hair," he said. He didn't look like the King in the North. He didn't look like the king of anything except maybe a vitamin D deficiency.

Harper stayed for a little while longer, and the two of them talked about other things, less heady stuff—North Pole gossip and what it was like to live in Florida. Then, after she'd gone home and left him drained from the extended social interaction, Oliver poured himself a bowl of popcorn and trudged upstairs. He sat on his bed and again noted the silence. It was even worse now, because now he wasn't just a guy sitting in a quiet room; he was a friendless asshole sitting in an empty room.

His phone buzzed with a message from proud_hoser. "There's an *Everybody Loves Raymond* marathon on TV. I just wasted half the day."

He sent her a smiley emoji, even though he actually felt

sad-face. As much as he dreamed about hanging out with her in real life—running through snowdrifts while trying to catch Stashes; sipping cider at Santabucks; kissing her in a dark room at a party, like how he'd caught Kevin Snow and Katie Murphy last night—his thing with proud_hoser was only good because they hadn't met in person. If she got to know the real him, she'd learn the truth—he was a jerk to everyone.

She said, "I was at a party last night. Harper Anderson's. You know her?"

His heart banged against his chest like it was trying to escape his rib cage. "I was there, too."

proud_hoser sent him the party favor emoji. "I scoured the place for you. I wish I had known you were there."

What if they had found each other last night? What if she had found him and they'd met at the party? He would've blown it, that's what would have happened. He would've gotten all self-deprecating and snarky. He wouldn't have known how to communicate to her that he really, really, desperately liked her. Or that he was terrified she wouldn't like him.

"I want to meet you," she said. "I want to know who you are."

His eyes grew heavy. "That's not a good idea."

"Why not?"

He ran through all the reasons why not in his head—he'd ruin it, he'd disappoint her, he was, point of fact, a total jerk to all humans. Instead he said, "We're the Grecian urn."

"Like the poem?" she asked. "About the scene on the vase where the guy is trying to get the girl?"

"Yeah, and the people on the vase will never actually get together. They're always and forever going to be pre-kiss." He blushed after typing the word "kiss." "It's all anticipation and excitement. You and I, right now, we're in the good part, before everything's revealed and it all goes to shit. And I want to stay here for a little bit longer." He'd stay here forever if he could.

But he knew this had a shelf-life, no matter what. The game would be over in a month. He'd either lose his connection to proud_hoser or she'd grow tired of the anonymity and he'd have to reveal his identity in order to keep chatting with her.

"It doesn't have to go to shit, does it?" she asked.

"Doesn't it always?" Oliver couldn't remember a time in his life when he hadn't caused a relationship to end badly, usually before it started. Like back in Florida, sophomore year, when he went to homecoming with a girl and spent the entire dance ignoring her because he didn't know if she liked him and he didn't want to let on that he was interested if she wasn't.

"Are you sure you're not Craig?" asked proud_hoser. "Were you lying to me before?"

"NO!" he said. "I'm not Craig."

"Then why can't we meet?"

"We will. I promise. Soon." In the meantime, he'd do what Harper suggested. He'd work on his people skills. He'd practice on Elena Chestnut.

"Okay fine, but tell me one tiny, little, concrete thing about yourself, one itty-bitty morsel I can obsess over for now."

He opened the metaphorical door just a tiny crack. "Okay...I hate cheese," he wrote. "I don't eat it. I tell people I'm allergic just so it scares them into not putting cheese on my stuff."

She wrote back almost immediately. "I can no longer speak to you. We're going to have to end this virtual relationship. Nice knowing you. Good-bye."

Oliver's heart started thumping again, this time from fear. She was kidding, probably, but what if she wasn't? What if she had some kind of thing where she truly could never be friends with someone who hated cheese? What if this, right here, was the last time he'd ever get to chat with proud_hoser?

She wrote back a few seconds later. "You know I'm going

to be checking out everyone's lunch in the cafeteria from now on, trying to figure out if it's you."

He hugged the phone to his chest for a moment, then responded, "I hope you do."

Chapter Seven

Elena was already in a bad mood when she arrived home on Monday afternoon.

It had been fish and chips day at school.

Fish and chips meant too many people in the cafeteria were eating cheese-free lunches, so she couldn't sniff out the non-cheese eaters. Her Stashiuk4Prez stalking attempt fell flat.

Then she had to meet Oliver at Santabucks for a quick tutoring session before his Latin quiz the next day. For some reason, he was unflappably pleasant to her. She'd say something snide to him, for instance, "Your handwriting looks like a serial killer's."

And he'd respond with a compliment, like "Yours is so straight and neat."

When she stood up to leave at the end of a half hour, he looked her right in the eye and said, "Thanks for working with me today, Elena."

She had no idea how to respond to that, so she bugged out her eyes and left the store, wondering what this new overly polite angle was all about. Was he trying to lull her into a false sense of security before dropping some bombshell? Well, she would not be lulled.

Even though she was wearing snow boots and not her gym shoes, Elena ran all the way home from Main Street—stopping to catch a few Stashes on the way. That little burst of exercise was enough to keep her from totally losing her mind until she reached her house.

There she found her mom in the kitchen, yelling into the phone. "We've never been late before…Okay, yes, 'until now,' but please, I need you to give us one more week!" She rushed through the last words. Then, "No?…*No*?…Okay, *fine*!" She stabbed at the end button on her phone and dropped her head into her hands.

"Mom?" Elena asked after a moment. She was fairly certain she wasn't supposed to have heard that.

Her mom glanced up, startled. "Honey, hi." She turned her back on Elena and wiped her eyes on her T-shirt.

"Is everything all right?"

Her mom turned around. She plastered a smile across her face that couldn't mask her red eyes. "It will be. Don't worry about it."

Of course she was worried. What else did her mom expect her to be? "What was that call about?"

Her mom shook her head, the Joker-esque, fake smile still on her lips. "It's really nothing. I'm glad you're here, though." She pulled out a chair at the kitchen table, sat down, and started flipping through her address book. "Your dad and I have decided to take a little trip, last minute."

"A vacation? Do we have money for that?"

Her mom's eyes were down on the book. "Nothing big, just going to see Aunt Patti in Wisconsin for a few days. It's been a while."

"She was just here for Christmas."

"It's been a while since we went to see her." Elena's mom sighed and rubbed her eyes. "We just need a few days away, okay? We'll leave Friday and come back Sunday. It's not up for discussion. Can you hold down the fort?"

Her mom's words slapped Elena across the cheek. She'd never seen her so frazzled before, so near the edge. "The fort? You mean, the store?" asked Elena. "You need me to watch that, too?"

Her mom sniffed. It was almost a laugh, like she had forgotten, momentarily, that the store even existed. "Yes, and the store." She frowned, her shoulders slumping. "Is that okay? I should've asked first. Are we ruining any big plans?"

Elena's mom ran a hand through her short, highlighted hair. Over the past few days, since Oliver Prince had cornered her and told her about their parents' maybe-past, Elena had hunted for photos around the house. She'd found pictures of her mom and dad, but not even one of Trip Prince. Back in the day, her mom had long, dark hair like Elena's. She was a totally different person now, from a completely different life. Her mom was a stranger to her now. "No big plans," Elena said.

She marched upstairs to her room and tossed her bag onto the bed, fuming, wondering why she was old enough to watch the store and the house and everything, but not old enough to be told what was going on. She knew her parents were having money troubles; that much was obvious. But apparently, it wasn't just their past her mom and dad liked to keep hidden from her. It was their present, too.

Her phone buzzed with a message from Stashiuk4Prez. Her fears and frustrations melted away, at least momentarily. This game, this guy, were the best distractions on the planet.

His message said, "Okay. Help me out here. Today I stood in front of the sports trophy case for my entire free period, staring at the track team."

"Why?" she asked.

"Trying to figure out which one was you."

She frowned. "I'm not on the track team." Though she used to be.

"I thought you were a runner."

A lump formed in her throat. "No time," she said. Then she added, with shaking fingers, "No money."

"That sucks."

"Yup." The tears poured out. It did suck. And it was something she'd never admitted before. She'd told Harper that she quit track and cross-country because she didn't like competing anymore. She didn't like the practices and all the travel. That was bullshit. She loved the competition. She loved all of it. The truth was, her parents needed her at the store, and they didn't have the funds to pay for fees and uniforms and equipment.

"I wish I could help," he said.

"Heh," she wrote back, "me, too."

"Can I start a donation campaign for you or something?"

She wrote back quickly, "NO." She didn't want anyone's charity. She never wanted that. This was her and her family's own private business. She said, "Thanks, but no. It wouldn't solve the time issue, would it?"

She watched the phone for almost a whole minute as she waited for him to finish writing. When he finally sent the message, it said, "I know it's a dumb thing to say, but I'm hugging you right now, mentally. Just know that."

She smiled to herself. Then she grabbed her pillow and clutched it tightly to her chest. With her entire being, she longed for him to be hugging her in real life right now. Since Stashiuk4Prez, a faceless avatar in the Stash Grab app, was the only person in the world she could open up to, she decided to keep that going, even at the risk of utter embarrassment. She told him, "I'm literally hugging my pillow right now, pretending it's you."

After she sent the text, she tossed her phone to the other side of the room and buried her blushing face in her hands, embarrassed as hell for typing that. She'd freaking told the guy she liked that she was hugging a pillow while imagining it was him. Elena would never hear from Stashiuk4Prez again after that. She'd completely ruined everything with that one stupid text.

Convinced that her maybe romance with Stashiuk4Prez was over, she crawled across the room to the phone. She didn't deserve to walk. Walking was for winners. Elena flipped over her phone. She nearly dropped it when she saw the new message alert. Stashiuk4Prez had written her back. Oh my God. He'd actually written her back. "I was literally hugging my pillow, too," he said, "but I was too embarrassed to say anything."

She had not scared him off. It was a miracle. Elena dared to push the limits one more time. She clicked on the heart emoji and stared at her unsent message for a few long seconds: a red heart, right there, ready to go. Then, with a deep breath, she hit send.

Two seconds later, he sent her the same heart back.

• • •

There was an assembly at school the next day, first thing in the morning.

Elena found a spot next to Harper in the auditorium; and then, right before the principal took the stage, Oliver Prince slid into the seat on Harper's other side.

"Hi Elena," he said.

She rolled her eyes and focused on the empty podium.

Harper whispered, "He said hi, Elena."

"Yeah?" Elena said.

"He's trying," Harper whispered even more softly.

Elena turned toward Oliver Prince, who was watching her with his stupid brown eyes, and said, "Why hello there, Oliver. How are you today? Marvelous, I'm sure."

She faced front again, but she heard Harper next to her say, "Good job." Out of the corner of her eye, Elena saw Harper pat his knee. So, she guessed that was still happening. And Harper was trying to get her new beau to buddy up to her best friend. Whatever.

The principal stepped on stage and announced, "We need to discuss the Stash Grab game." Mrs. Olsen peered down at all of them from behind the glare of her glasses. "I love that you're all so involved in this and that it's getting you all outside and moving in the dead of winter, but I want you to stay smart." She held out a hand toward the front row. "Stand up please, Mr. Shaw. Show them your hands."

Jimmy Shaw, the freshman who'd once been so captivated by the Stash Grab game that he'd bumped right into Elena, stood up and turned around. Both of his hands were completely bandaged.

"Frostbite," said Mrs. Olsen. "Mr. Shaw stayed out for three hours after dark this weekend, hunting for Stashes, while wearing no mittens." She motioned for him to sit down.

"Ridiculous," Elena muttered. She turned toward Oliver. "You're responsible, you know. I sure hope his family doesn't sue you."

"They won't," he said. "My dad already gave them a bunch of hockey equipment."

She folded her arms. "That's so Prince, buying off your enemies, taking no responsibility for anything."

Mrs. Olsen leaned into the mic. "Mr. Shaw is not the only Stash Grab casualty. Mrs. Page broke her wrist. My own assistant, Katie, got a black eye when someone whipped a snowball at her to keep her from grabbing a Stash." The principal shook her head. "We are better than this, North Pole High. I want you to dial it down. You're competing for some plane tickets, not a tour of Wonka's chocolate factory."

She dismissed them all after that.

At lunch—beef stew, again no cheese—the students started getting rebellious.

"She can't tell us how to play," Kevin Snow complained, ripping off a big hunk of bread from his baguette. "We can stay out all night if we want to."

"Which is moot," said Harper, "because the Stashes stop popping up after eleven and don't show up again until six in the morning."

Danny put his arm around Star's shoulders. "We should have, like, an all-night Stash hunt party just to stick it to Mrs. Olsen."

"Yeah," Star and Kevin agreed.

"Again," said Harper. "No overnight Stashes. We'd have to have, like, a regular party that ended at eleven."

An idea started to form in Elena's head.

Chestnut's should host that party.

Why should the Princes be the only ones to profit from Stash Grab? Sure, it was their thing, but she'd seen other stores getting in on it around town. Santabucks had some Stash Grab drink specials—like Stan Stashiuk's favorite toasted coconut mocha. The video store had started showing hockey movies at their usual Saturday night movie viewing. They also had hot apple cider on hand all day long, for any Stash Grab player who needed a warm-up.

Why shouldn't Chestnut's get in on the game? And with her parents out of town, it was the perfect time to jump in. It might give the store just the boost it needed.

After school, Elena ran home and sat down at her parents' desk in the den. She pulled out the town directory and, with a sour face, dialed Craig's number. He answered on the first ring, because of course he did. "Craig Cooper," he said.

"Hi, Craig." She used her most professional voice. "It's Elena Chestnut."

There was a pause. Then he said, "I work at Prince's now."

She sighed. "I know, and thank you for your loyalty, *Craig*."

"I have to go where the money is. You understand that, Elena."

Sure, but she wouldn't tell him that. "You're not working this Friday night, are you?"

There was a pause. "Elena," he said, "you're too young for me."

Elena gagged, nearly retching onto her phone. "This is business, Craig, not personal."

"Well, in that case, no. I'm not working."

"Great," said Elena, crossing her fingers for luck. "I have a proposition for you, then. How about you come to Chestnut's on Friday night and DJ for me? We're throwing a little party at the store."

"What?" he asked. "Why? This feels like a conflict of interest."

"What are you, an attorney? It's not a conflict of interest."

"How much do I get?"

"Nothing, Craig. You get nothing. You were one of our loyal customers for years, and you work at Prince's now. You owe us one night of your time."

Elena could almost feel his disgusted eye-roll over the phone. She'd seen it many times before. "All right," he said with a sigh. "I'll do it."

"Thank you."

She hung up the phone before he could change his mind and started crafting an invite on the computer. Chestnut's was throwing a Stash Grab Dash until midnight on Friday night. Food, hot cocoa, big fun, big prizes.

She sent it to everyone in her email list, and everyone in the town directory and the high school book. She paused when she got to the Princes, wondering if she should invite Oliver and Regina. She hesitated a minute, then typed in their addresses. *They should come*, she thought. *They should see firsthand that Chestnut's is not going under any time soon.*

She sent the invite and sat back, waiting for the RSVPs to roll in.

. . .

"You're going," said Harper.

"I'm really not," Oliver told her. He was working at Prince's on Wednesday after school. No one was in the store, so he had occupied the comfy desk chair in the office, feet up on the desk, to talk on the phone to Harper. She was trying to get him to click "yes" on the invite from Elena.

"This party is a great social opportunity. Everyone's going to be there, running around, catching Stashes. There will be so much going on, you'll barely have to talk to anyone."

"It feels like a personal affront," he said, tapping a pencil on the desk.

"What do you mean?"

"I bet she only invited me to rub it in, to be like, 'Hey, come witness my family's store enjoying the fruits of Oliver's labor and he can't do anything about it.'"

"I guarantee you that wasn't her thought process. Elena's not vindictive like that."

"You say that, but why invite me if not to make me feel like shit? She hates me. I've tried being nice to her—you've seen it." She had been out on Main Street earlier that afternoon, carrying a sack of groceries from Ludlum's. He'd said hello. She'd told him to devour a bag full of male genitalia.

"Elena's not that nasty a person," Harper said.

Oliver didn't know what Elena was, but he knew he didn't care to investigate further. He'd seen enough. He was being forced to spend time with her during their tutoring sessions, but that was where he drew the line. "I'm not going," he said again.

"It's only Wednesday. Don't make any decisions y—"

Harper was cut off as the front doorbell ripped through the store. A customer. First one all afternoon, actually. Oh, if Elena could see Prince's now. The January lull in North Pole was real, and Prince's Sporting Goods was feeling the effects. "Harper, I have to go—"

But he'd barely gotten the words out when he heard a man growl, "Whatever you're doing, Trip, stop it."

Oliver pressed the eend button on his phone and held his breath.

"That's rich, coming from you." It was Oliver's dad.

"It's not even remotely the same situation," the other man said. "Stop. Calling. My. Wife."

Oliver slid off the chair and slithered over to the office door to hide behind it. He could've made his presence known, but that would've meant inserting himself into whatever his dad and this man were arguing about, and Oliver was not a meddler.

"Your wife called me, Tom," said Trip.

Oliver's heart beat faster. Tom. Tom Chestnut. Elena's dad.

Both he and Trip sounded too enraged to worry about who might be listening in on their conversation. "Bullshit," Tom said. "Why would she call you?"

"I don't know," Trip said. "I didn't call her back. Check her phone, because apparently that's something you do. She called me. I didn't call her back."

"Why would she—?"

"Maybe she realized she picked the wrong guy." Trip

laughed.

Oliver's phone buzzed. A message from Harper. *You okay?*

He shut off the screen and shoved the phone into his pocket.

"That's low, Trip," Tom said.

"Of course *you* know what low is. You're the king of low. You're the one who eloped with my fiancée."

Oliver clamped his hand over his mouth. Tom Chestnut eloped with Oliver's dad's fiancée?

"Again, Trip, that was twenty years ago. A lifetime ago. We both have kids now. We're happily married."

Trip didn't respond. Oliver noted the silence.

"Wait a minute," said Trip. "Where is everyone?" He paused, seemingly realizing that he and Tom Chestnut should not be alone in an open retail establishment. "Oliver? Are you here?"

Sheepishly, Oliver stood up from his crouch and tiptoed out of the office. "I was on the phone in there—"

"Fine, fine," Trip said. "Tom was just leaving."

Mr. Chestnut nodded. "It's true. I was. So long, Trip."

Oliver and his dad watched in silence as Tom Chestnut left the store.

Then Trip let out a huge sigh. "Ugh." He walked over to the coffee bar and poured himself a cup.

Oliver stood there for a moment, waiting for an explanation, some easily digestible sound bite that would shed a light on everything. His dad had been engaged before— apparently to Elena's mom, who may or may not have called Trip on the phone recently. Oliver needed more information to go on. "Dad, did Mrs. Chestnut call you?"

His dad poured creamer into his cup. "She did."

"And you didn't call her back?" The picture of his dad and Elena's mom kept popping into Oliver's mind. He remembered his mom's questions about why Trip had wanted to come back here and why it would be awkward for Elena Chestnut to tutor their son. Oliver had let all those comments soar over his head, because he was too concerned about his own garbage to catch their meaning. But Regina was right. Things were bad between their parents, and he should be worried.

Trip deflected the question. "None of this is your business."

"You didn't call her, right?" This was another conversation above Oliver's pay grade. He had never been in a serious relationship before — and he'd definitely never been married — but he did know it was probably not a great idea for his dad to be calling his ex-fiancée, especially if her current husband wasn't too keen on the idea.

"Oliver, did you start stocking the swimming gear like I asked you to? Spring break is only a few weeks away."

Oliver nodded. "Yeah, it's done."

"Good." Trip put a lid on his cup, which he raised in salute. "See you at home."

Oliver watched as his dad left, heading in the exact opposite direction of their house.

Knees weak, he walked back into the office and sat in the chair. He stared at the wall for a moment. What did it mean that Trip didn't answer the question about calling Mrs. Chestnut? What did it mean that he said he was going home, but then turned the other way? Maybe he was just running some errands. That was probably it. He had to pick something up at the bakery or the flower shop.

Oliver pulled the infamous photo album out of the bottom desk drawer and turned right to the picture of his dad and Elena's mom, which he'd replaced after he showed it to Elena. They were definitely happy and obviously in love. He couldn't for the life of him remember his own mom and dad looking at each other like that.

Oliver peered closer at the photo. There was someone in the background, someone who was standing a bit behind them, a little out of focus, his arms folded across his chest. He was smiling, too.

Though he had a few extra pounds on him and a bit more hair then, it was clearly Tom Chestnut.

He flipped to the front of the album. There were some pictures he'd glossed over at first—ones from when his dad was a young kid, ones that had been meaningless to Oliver at first glance. There were several shots of Trip with the same boy, a boy with dark brown hair and bright blue eyes. Oliver pulled one of the pictures off the page and checked the back. *Trip and Tom, age 10.* And toward the end of the book, there were several of his college graduation. One was of him and just Tom Chestnut, with their arms around each other's shoulders.

They had been friends. Good friends, probably. At any rate, they'd known each other for a very long time.

His dad had put his trust in someone—two people, really—and had his heart broken. He'd held onto that grudge for twenty years. He'd taught Oliver and Regina to hate the Chestnuts. He'd never wavered in his unflinching desire to see bad things happen to them.

And now his dad was talking—maybe—to Elena's mom again.

Oliver pulled out his phone and composed a message to proud_hoser. "Hey," he said, staring at the picture of his dad and Elena's parents at their college graduation. "What if you had information about someone else that could possibly ruin their life? Would you tell them?"

She wrote back, "Whoa. Wow. Would the person knowing make a difference? Like would they be able to do anything about it?"

"I don't know." If he and Elena got on the same page, perhaps they could work together to keep his dad and her mom away from each other. "Possibly," he said. "Though it could be a real 'shoot-the-messenger' type situation."

"Is this person close to you? Would you feel bad burning this bridge?" she asked.

"Hahaha," he wrote back right away. "No. There is no bridge."

"Then I think it's a no-brainer. If the person gets pissed, no big deal. You lose nothing, and you still come off like the good guy in the situation, having done the right thing."

Oliver put the photo album and his phone away and skulked to the front of the store. It was dark outside, and, across the street, Chestnut's was lit up from the inside. Elena and her dad were alone in the shop. He stood behind the register, and she was fiddling with the window display.

Her mom was nowhere to be seen.

And Trip Prince had turned in the opposite direction of home when he'd left the store.

Elena glanced up and her eyes met Oliver's.

proud_hoser was right. Oliver had to bite the bullet and tell Elena what was going on, even though she might literally shoot the messenger. Oliver would want to know, if the situations were reversed.

When Elena looked over, Oliver raised his hand in greeting. Maybe he could wave her over, and they could talk about their parents here, tonight, alone. But she flipped him the bird, turned away, and faded deeper into her family's store.

She was not going to make this easy on him, was she?

Chapter Eight

"Check one. Sibilance. Sibilance."

"Craig, can you keep it down?" Elena was standing inside Chestnut's, counting the chairs she'd set up around the floor. She had cleared away a big space in the middle, pushing some of the shelves to the side, and had lined up more seating along the perimeter. They were expecting at least forty people, and those were just the ones who'd RSVP-ed. Who knew who might crawl in off the street?

"I have to make sure the mic is working properly," Craig retorted. He stood behind a podium next to the refreshments table and started unzipping one of the thermal bags protecting the pizza.

Elena ran over and swatted his hand away. "That's for the guests!"

"I am a guest," he said. "It's not like you're paying me to be here."

"I know," she said. "Just…wait. Have some coffee." She gestured toward the other end of the table, where Danny Garland had set up two percolators (one regular and one decaf), a carafe of hot cocoa, and a tower of paper cups.

He scowled as he hiked up his mom jeans. "Coffee and pizza? Unorthodox."

"Shut up," she said. "I don't know. There's pop and water, too, in the coolers under the table."

The pizza was a last-minute addition. She had planned on just coffee and hot chocolate, maybe some pastries, which Danny's mom had offered to donate. But then the pizzeria in town, Pie-lent Night, offered to supply food and pop at no cost. Elena just had to advertise their business. On the off-chance that Stashiuk4Prez might show up, she'd used her own tutoring money to buy a few cheese-free pizzas as a test. It was worth a shot.

At seven o'clock sharp, she threw open the door and a throng of people pushed into Chestnut's. The entire town was there—Danny, Star, Kevin, and Brian; Mags, Dolores, and Frank; Mayor Sandoval, Dinesh, and Sam. The entire high school soccer team showed up *en masse*. Maurice, the guy who owned the video store, had shut down for the night. The only people who weren't there, from what Elena could see, were the Princes. And Harper.

Her heart sunk for a second at Harper's absence. Harper had promised she'd be here, she'd vowed to come after Elena had gone to her, begging for any cast-off prizes the Andersons might be able to provide for the Stash Grab Dash. Harper had come through with some NBA tickets and said she'd show up well before the start of the event. Elena longed to text Harper, to find out where she was, but she didn't have time to wallow in her sadness. The folks who were milling around, waiting in line to report their current Stash Grab scores to Craig, actually started shopping, and she suddenly became very busy.

Relieved, Elena finally spotted Harper when the Stash Grab Dash was about to start and she had joined Craig up at the DJ booth. But when she saw that her best friend was out in the crowd laughing and whispering with Oliver Prince, all the good vibes fled Elena's body.

Whenever he wasn't muttering in Harper's ear, Oliver was watching Elena with these infuriating hangdog eyes. Why was he here at all? He'd responded "no" to the invitation. Was he hoping to throw her off her game? To laugh at her little event? Was he somehow going to bogart the night and get people to shop at Prince's instead? Elena was not about to let that happen. She wouldn't give him the opportunity. She'd make sure to stay the hell away from Oliver Prince all night. She was too busy for his nonsense, anyway.

She grabbed Craig's microphone and held it a few inches from her face, trying to avoid Craig's cooties. She'd spotted him slobbering all over the mic during setup. "Welcome, everybody, to Chestnut's first ever Stash Grab Dash."

The crowd cheered.

"Here's how it works. You all should've given Craig your current Stash Grab scores by now. He has officially recorded all the numbers."

Craig held up a poster board with everyone's current scores written on it. He waved his hand in front of the sign with a flourish, like a game show spokesmodel.

"On my whistle," Elena said, "you will have one hour to run around town catching Stashes. You must be back here in sixty minutes—exactly—in order to win. If you're late, you're out of luck. This is one of those moments in your life where it's important to be on time, Danny Garland."

Everyone laughed.

"I showed up late for one basketball game, one time!" Danny said.

"All the basketball games, all the time," Kevin corrected him with a friendly pat on the shoulder.

"When you return, Craig and I will tally up the scores.

Whoever earns the most Stash points within the hour is the big winner, and we have a fabulous prize for you—two floor seats to a Timberwolves game, courtesy of Sam and Harper's dad, Mr. Anderson. For the rest of you, when you get back, we'll have food and music, and you can take your Stash Grab score and divide it by one thousand. We'll let you take that percentage off one item—any item—in Chestnut's!"

The room erupted in applause.

"On your mark!"

The people in the room prepared to dash out. Elena said a quick prayer that no one got trampled or gravely injured. She hadn't considered the possibility that someone might hurt themselves. Oh well. Too late now.

"Get set!" She paused, her heart thumping, then she blew hard into a whistle she'd pilfered from the referee section of the shop.

The entire store emptied on her cue. There was quite a bottleneck at the actual door, and flop sweat formed on Elena's brow, but no one was seriously hurt. Dinesh's hand may have gotten pinched in the door, but he didn't seem too concerned about it. He took off running as soon as he hit the sidewalk.

Alone in the store, Craig stared at Elena, hopping from foot to foot.

"Do you need me?" he asked, eyes darting to the street.

"Go, Craig," she said. "Have fun."

Elena watched as he, too, barreled out of the store. She wished she could join the horde—she could've used a full hour of Stash Grabbing, because she still really wanted those tickets—but someone had to stay behind and "hold down the fort," as per her mother's request. She wasn't keeping her Stash Grabbing on the down low anymore. She didn't advertise it, and her parents still didn't know, but after Danny Garland caught her catching Stashes in Santabucks, trying to hide her gameplay was futile.

She started to make her way back to the register when a voice from the fishing aisle said, "Impressive event." Oliver Prince stepped out from the shadows like Nosferatu.

"What are you doing here?" She folded her arms.

He ducked his chin sheepishly, but he didn't come any closer. "Harper," he said with a slight grin. "She's trying to get me to be more social."

Elena gestured toward the door. "Well, everybody's out there."

"I know, but…I wanted to talk to you about something."

She rested her hands on her hips. "Yeah?"

Now he did step closer. "You should sit down."

Though his wide, frightened eyes scared the crap out of her, Elena stood her ground. "I'm fine." This conversation was giving her a weird sense of déjà vu.

"Your call." Oliver shrugged. "I wanted to let you know your dad came into Prince's the other day."

That was news. Her dad hadn't been inside Prince's store in…to her knowledge he'd never stepped foot inside Prince's store.

"He and my dad were fighting," said Oliver, nodding toward the street, toward Prince's, like he was trying to set the scene. "I was in the office, and they didn't know I was there, so I listened in." He paused. "Did you know that my dad used to be engaged to your mom?"

The words kicked the wind out of her, because of the news itself and also because of the sense of dread she still couldn't place. Elena shrugged. "Yup," she lied.

He frowned. "You knew?"

"Everyone knows." She would not share confidences with Oliver Prince, and she would not let him assume he'd known something before she did.

"Well, I didn't," he said. "So you knew that your dad and

my dad used to be friends?"

She braced herself, tightening the muscles in her legs to stay strong and upright. Oliver kept dropping bombshells at her feet, all these little bits of information tying her family to the Princes. "I knew that."

From across the room, he searched her face—trying to assess whether or not she was telling the truth. "That's old news, I suppose, but…um…what's been happening recently is, apparently, your mom has been calling my dad and your dad's not happy about it." He held up his hands in surrender. "Don't shoot the messenger."

"Whoa. What?"

"Your mom has been calling my dad."

Elena shook her head. "Not that. The last part."

"Don't shoot the messenger?"

"That's it." Blinking, she put a hand to her heart, which was beating fast. Her rib cage squeezed the air from her lungs.

Needing a distraction, Elena stepped over to the refreshments table and busied herself setting up the food. "Don't shoot the messenger" was what Stashiuk4Prez had said the other day, an odd little conversation they'd had while she was painting her nails, one she'd barely given a second thought to since. Stashiuk4Prez had bad news to tell someone, and now here was Oliver Prince, standing in front of her, telling her that their parents might be hooking up. He was the messenger. And, yes, she wanted to shoot him.

She squatted and lined up some cans of pop at one end. It couldn't be. There was no way Oliver Prince and Stashiuk4Prez were the same person. The universe was simply not that cruel.

A nearby rustle indicated that Oliver had joined her at the table and had started unzipping the thermal bags of pizza. "My dad claims he didn't call her back," said Oliver. "But when he left Prince's and said he was going home, he turned in the opposite direction. I'm not sure where he went—"

That was enough. Elena jumped up from her crouch. She was not about to listen to another word of this. This was supposed to be her night, and now here he was, ruining *everything*. "You don't have to help." She wrestled a box of pizza away from him. "I don't *need* your help."

"I know...I'm just..." He backed away from the table. "Aren't you worried our parents are having an affair?"

She folded her arms. "Nope." That was currently the least of her worries. "Maybe your mom and dad are having problems, but mine are not. Everything's fine. You're only here to ruin things."

He shook his head. "I'm really not. Elena, I thought we could—"

"There is no 'we,' Oliver Prince." She shuddered, recalling every conversation she'd had with Stashiuk4Prez over the past few weeks. "There is my family and there is your family, and we've all done just splendidly for the past several decades, steering clear of each other. Let's not ruin the streak."

He raised his eyebrows. "You're being ridiculous."

"I'm being ridiculous?" She stepped toward him and poked him in the chest. "You're the one who came here, to my store, on the night of my big event and decided to drop a deuce on it by telling me you think our parents are hooking up. Why? Why now? Why couldn't you have waited until tomorrow or the next time I tutor you or something? It's because you're jealous I'm hosting this contest and you have to sit on the sidelines watching it happen."

"Yeah, I'm jealous of you, Elena." His words oozed with sarcasm and his brown eyes flashed orange from the Christmas lights that still framed Chestnut's front window. This was the Oliver Prince she knew and loathed. This was the guy she was used to. There was no way this ogre was the same guy she'd poured her heart out to via the Stash Grab app. "Oh, I'm so jealous that you're running a failing store that could close at any moment. I'm dripping with envy, and not at all smug, that you had to piggyback on the thing I created just to keep your store afloat for another—what?—week or two?"

"We're doing just fine."

"Sure you are." He glanced around at the empty store. "The only way you could get anyone in here tonight was by promising them prizes and discounts—because of my game."

Elena stepped toward him, straightening her spine to raise herself to his eye level. She was not going to let him bring her down. Not tonight. Tonight was her night. "You're terrible, Oliver Prince. You are the most arrogant, self-centered—"

He bent down until they were almost nose to nose. A wave of heat—from anger only, obviously—ran up Elena's spine. He said, "I have been trying to be nicer to you. I've said hello, I've been pleasant. You've just gotten meaner."

"You were mocking me."

"I was not." He ran his fingers through his thick auburn hair, something he did when he was nervous or particularly frustrated. He did this a lot during their tutoring sessions. "I was working against my better instincts to be nicer to you. Harper insisted you were someone worth knowing. She was so, so fucking wrong."

Elena pursed her lips. This jackass. What did he know?

He kept going. "I came here tonight for one reason only—to tell you about our parents, because it felt like the right thing to do. Why tonight?" He held up his hand and ticked off the reasons. His fingers were long but thick, with perfectly clean nails. When it hit her that she was drooling over Oliver Prince's hands—how pathetic—she focused on his eyes instead, which were swirling brown hurricanes, dead set on destroying her. Well, not if she destroyed him first.

"I had to do it tonight," he said, "because when I caught your eye on Wednesday, you gave me the finger. When I tried to talk to you during lunch, you turned away and struck up a conversation with Star. When I attempted to bring it up during our tutoring session yesterday, you pretended to get a very important text. I have been running myself ragged trying to be decent to you, and you have given me nothing."

"Well, you—" She wracked her brain, hunting for something she could toss back at him, some grievous sin he'd committed against her in the past few weeks. She could come up with nothing. He was right. He had been nice. He had been greeting her kindly and doing his work before and during their tutoring appointments. He even offered her an apple at lunch the other day when she said she was starving, and she told him to go choke on it. She put her hands on her hips and shot daggers into his eyes. "Well, you," she repeated, "are a *Prince*." His last name tasted bitter in her mouth.

"And you," he said, "are kind of a pain in the butt, which, Chestnut or not, I guess is just who you are."

Her nostrils flared. She pointed to the door. "Get out."

"Gladly." Then he reached past her. She caught a whiff of cold sweat and cloves under the lingering scent of Harper's Obsession perfume. Then Elena watched as Oliver grabbed a slice of the cheese-less pizza she'd bought specifically for Stashiuk4Prez, and held it up like a toast before disappearing into the night.

. . .

Oliver ran into Harper just off Main Street on his way back home. On a normal evening, he, the Florida boy, would've been jumping up and down to fight against the cold, but tonight his righteous indignation kept him warm. He, Oliver, had done the noble thing. He had attempted to ally forces with Elena Chestnut, and she had rejected him. That was on her. Oliver was completely and totally on the right side of history here.

"Where are you going?" Harper panted after him.

"Home." He gnawed a bit of the cheese-less pizza he'd stolen from Elena's store. "Or something. I don't know. Maybe I'll run a marathon or dance in the moonlight. A weight has been lifted from my shoulders."

"That's...good? And bizarre." Harper paused to grab a Stash in front of the town hall and then ran to catch up.

"It is good." He puffed some air from his nose, and it swirled around him like smoke. "I tried talking to Elena tonight, and she..." He shook his head. "I was always so sure I was the one who had problems relating to other people, but now I know. It's not me. It's her. She's the one who sucks." He popped the last bit of crust into his mouth.

"She doesn't, though," whined Harper.

"Oh, you say that, but you're wrong."

"It'd make my life so much easier if you two would just get along!"

Swallowing his mouthful of pizza, he nodded in the direction of Chestnut's Sporting Goods. "Tell that to her."

"You just have to—"

"I don't 'have to' anything." Oliver held his hands wide, welcoming peace and tranquility into his universe. "I did my part. I tried to be the nice guy, to do the right thing, and she told me to go screw myself. I absolve myself of any feelings of social inadequacy. I'm not the problem. It's Elena Chestnut."

"Oliver!" Harper shouted after him, but he took off skipping, excited by his revelation. Oliver was perfectly capable of making friends. He'd made friends with Harper, after all. The only person he couldn't befriend was Elena Chestnut, and that was totally, 100 percent fine.

His phone buzzed, and he pulled off a mitten with his teeth to check it. There was a message from proud_hoser, and the sight of her name lit him up from the inside.

He read the text. She asked, "Are you having a good night?"

Grinning, he wrote, "Fanfreakingtastic." Then he spun around, wondering if she was part of the crowd running up and down Main Street—catching Stashes outside the barbershop or in the park. Was she alone? With friends? Had she stayed home? His stomach knotted. What if he met her tonight? It would be the optimal time. He was invincible right now.

"Why so fantastic?" she asked.

"Oh, I took your advice and told my mortal enemy the news I'd uncovered. She bit my head off, as I figured she might; but I'm feeling great, because I did the right thing." He waved at Bobbi Moore, owner of the flower shop in town, Holly and Ivy. She was marching over, dog leash in hand.

"You have a mortal enemy?" asked proud_hoser. "A girl?"

"The evilest witch in all the land."

He shoved his phone into his pocket and greeted the florist. "Hi, Bobbi."

"I wanted to talk to you." Her pinched face glared up at him. "Your little game. It's causing problems."

"I'm sorry about that." Oliver watched Bobbi's dog take a dump on the snow covering the lawn outside the town hall. Bobbi made no move to pick it up.

"There's a…what's it called?…a Stash?…in my backyard," she said. "People keep sneaking in late at night, waking up my dogs."

Oliver grinned. "That's too bad."

"It's not funny," said Bobbi. "They knocked over half my fence!"

"That's awful." But it was good news for Oliver. If Regina was sleeping on the job, maybe Oliver could talk his dad into giving him his computer back. Everything was coming up Oliver tonight.

"And Reverend Michaels?" Bobbi continued. "He said that a Stash popped up right in the middle of Sunday services last weekend. Tammy Cortez was singing the psalm and then—boom—everyone's phones started buzzing and chirping. It was a disaster, to hear him tell it. Fix it, or I'm going to the sheriff." She pursed her lips.

Sheriff Parsons was one of the most ardent Stash Grab players in town. He was probably one of the people breaking into Bobbi Moore's yard every night. "I'll tell my sister." Oliver rolled his eyes. "She's the one in charge."

"I don't care who's in charge," said Bobbi. "I just care that it gets taken care of. Now."

Oliver saluted her and bounced toward home, excited to tell his dad that Regina was pissing people off, that he, Oliver, should regain control of the game. He had so many ideas to implement—new, better coupons, stealing Elena's idea for the Stash Grab-related percentage off, hosting a Stash hunt of their own. He was ready to take this town by storm.

When he reached his house, he yanked off a glove and pulled out his phone. Tonight was his lucky night, and if he was ever going to take this risk, now was the time. He took a deep breath, his hands shaking, and composed a message to proud_ hoser. Then, noticing a few nervous typos, he erased his words and tried again—slowly, methodically, typing each letter one by one. "Hey," he said, "will you go to the Valentine's dance with me? Assuming you don't already have a date."

He'd expected her to write back immediately, because that's how his night was going, but she didn't. A lump in his throat, he fixed his eyes on his phone, which lay silent in his palm for a full three minutes and then another two. Begrudgingly, he gave up and shoved the phone into his pocket. Maybe his luck had run out. Maybe he'd pushed it too far.

But finally, a few hours later, just as Oliver was about to drift off into sleep, proud_hoser responded. "Yes! But let's meet there. I'll be wearing a yellow dress."

Relieved, Oliver wrote back frantically, not even worrying about typos or proper grammar this time. "And Ill bring u a yellow rose."

"It's a date," proud_hoser told him.

Sighing, Oliver clutched his phone to his chest and flopped backward onto his pillow. He closed his eyes, a grin still playing on his lips, and he dreamed of proud_hoser, whoever she might be, all night.

Chapter Nine

When all was said and done, the Stash Grab Dash at Chestnut's had brought in more money in one night than they'd seen in a while, though Elena could hardly enjoy her success.

She couldn't remember a time when the store was that full or the cash register was that busy. After the actual Stash Grabbing portion of the night had ended, everyone swarmed back into Chestnut's to eat, dance, and shop. She gave the basketball tickets to Dinesh, who had managed to earn the highest number of Stash points in an hour, and then she spent the rest of the night ringing people up. Everyone in attendance used their Stash Grab discount, and the biggest markdown she had to give was to Craig at 48 percent.

Elena had to admit the event also provided a good distraction from Oliver Prince, Stashiuk4Prez, and the cheeseless pizza.

After he'd left, she'd stood frozen in the middle of the floor, the garlicky odor from the Pie-lent Night bags filling her nostrils. Oliver Prince had come into her store that evening with the intention of breaking some bad news, he'd used the phrase "shoot the messenger," and he'd grabbed a slice of cheese-less pizza. Each detail on its own meant nothing, but together they added up to one logical and horrific conclusion: Oliver Prince was Stashiuk4Prez.

To test her theory, Elena messaged Stashiuk4Prez. "Are you having a good night?"

He wrote her back right away, telling her about his mortal enemy (a girl), and how he'd done the right thing, and how this chick was the "evilest witch in all the land."

When she saw that last message, Elena shut off her phone and tossed it aside, fuming. Evil? That guy hadn't seen evil yet.

She kept busy after that, arranging the food, making sure the chairs were set up properly. She plastered on a happy face for the customers and did a jig of joy when she counted the receipts at the end of the night, but lurking underneath the success-related happiness were pure anger and humiliation.

Elena had planned on heading home to her empty house after the event and hopping on the treadmill for an hour or so to run off her rage and confusion, but she found Harper waiting around on Main Street for her to close the store.

"What did you say to Oliver?" she asked as Elena locked the door.

"Were you waiting out here for me?" Elena shivered from the cold this time and not because of the incessant little aftershocks from the news that Oliver Prince and Stashiuk4Prez were one in the same. "It's freezing."

"I've only been out here for a minute," said Harper, falling in step with her. "I went to Oliver's house after the party to talk to him, but he was in no mood. Then I came back here and saw you sweeping. I obviously wanted nothing to do with that, so I went to Santabucks and got a hot cocoa instead." She raised her cup. "So, what did you say to him?"

"I—" It hit Elena then that there was even more to this Stashiuk4Prez/Oliver situation than she'd first realized. If

Oliver really was the guy she'd been chatting with, then Elena had inadvertently spent the past few weeks flirting with her best friend's crush. God, she was a horrible person. "What's going on between you two?" she asked.

"Between me and Oliver?" said Harper.

"Yeah, do you still like him?" The girls waved at Dottie in the bakery as they passed the Spruce Street store on the way to Elena's house.

"Do I still like Oliver?"

"Uh, yeah," said Elena. "That's not a hard question, is it?"

"No, but…" Harper stopped in her tracks.

Elena turned around to face her, pulling her scarf over her mouth. "Come on. This isn't stop-and-chat kind of weather."

"But it's a stop-and-chat conversation."

Elena bounced up and down to warm up.

Harper sucked in a breath. "It's not Oliver Prince I like. It's his sister."

Elena forgot all about Oliver, the cheese-free pizza, and the cold wind whipping at her cheeks. She couldn't speak. She was without speech. A sound came out of her mouth like, "Buhhhh."

"I know it sounds ludicrous," said Harper, "but we kind of…hooked up during the school ski trip and…I sort of wanted more, but she didn't—though we're cool, it's fine… now." Harper gulped. "But the thing is, it wasn't a one-time thing for me, or I don't want it to be. I've been wandering around for weeks, trying to figure it out, and, well, I have." She paused. "I like girls."

"You dated, like, the entire football team," Elena said.

"I know." Harper laughed, shrugging. "Smoke screen, I guess."

Elena blinked back tears that might have been from the wind, or they might have been from the fact that her best friend had been going through all this without her.

"I'm sorry I didn't tell you," said Harper.

Elena shook her head, getting a grip on the situation. "You had every right not to. It was your news to reveal on your timetable. But I mean…" She was trying to figure out a delicate way to ask this. "It's just…is it me? Did you feel like you couldn't come to *me*?" Maybe Oliver was onto something. Maybe Elena actually was a horrible person.

Harper pulled her into a hug. "No. No, of course not. I just needed time." She leaned back and stared Elena straight in the eye. "And it seemed like a huge step, coming out to my best friend; like that would make it real, and I wasn't ready for it to be real." She laughed. "I guess it's real." She nodded down the street. "Now, let's keep walking, because it's cold as shit."

The pit in Elena's stomach kept growing. She swallowed hard to keep it from rising to her throat. She'd always considered herself to be tough and independent and like she could handle anything anyone threw at her. But tonight kept testing that. Everything was changing. Her world was spinning off its axis. Her best friend had hooked up with a Prince twin—the girl Prince twin—weeks ago and hadn't told her. And though Elena had managed to bring in some money at Chestnut's tonight, who knew if it was enough? Her parents' business was still failing. And her mom might be having an affair. The fact that she'd spent the past several weeks accidentally romancing her sworn enemy with her words was really the least of Elena's worries at this point.

"Did Oliver know?" she managed to choke out.

Harper was silent for a moment. Elena turned to see her friend's face, but a fluffy white muffler obstructed her view. "Don't get mad," she said. "He did, but not because I told him. That was all Regina."

"I'm not mad," said Elena. Why did everyone assume she was angry all the time?

"He was honestly great about the whole thing, so supportive. I know he comes off as kind of a loner jerk, but he's not that bad."

"Hmph," said Elena. Oliver had Harper fooled.

"He's really a decent guy," insisted Harper. "I've been trying to get him to work on being nicer to people—especially you—and he tried so hard." Elena caught the accusatory tone. Harper was laying it on pretty thick.

"He's a Prince," Elena said. That should've been excuse enough.

"I know I'm newish to town," said Harper, "but hasn't this feud gone on long enough?"

"No." Elena unlocked the front door to her house. "Forever wouldn't be long enough."

She dropped her keys on the table next to the door and commenced removing all her layers of outerwear. "You staying over?" Elena asked.

"You finally caught on." Harper reached into her bag and pulled out a DVD from the video store—*The Greasy Strangler*.

"Ew," Elena said, eyeing the cover. "That looks... unpleasant."

Harper assessed the DVD box, shrugging. "Sam says it's great, I don't know. He shoved it into my hands."

The two girls plodded up to Elena's room. Though she'd planned to jump on the treadmill for a run, Elena's legs felt like bags of lead and her eyes weren't much lighter. Harper's company and a dumb movie were what just she needed right now.

Harper flopped onto the bed and clicked play on the remote before turning on her phone. "Any Stashes on your property?" she asked.

"I don't think so." Elena's own phone weighed heavy in her jeans pocket. She wondered if Oliver had written her back, if he had any more choice insults for his mortal enemy, the evilest witch in town. "Hey," she said, "did you know Oliver is playing his own game? Like, he has an account and is out there catching Stashes with everyone else. Is he trying to skew the results in some way?" The thought had occurred to her earlier, while she was cleaning up Chestnut's after the Stash Grab Dash.

Harper chuckled. "Nah. He's keeping tabs on Regina, looking for glitches, places where she may have fucked up. She hasn't really fucked up, which annoys him to no end."

"Oh."

Harper's eyes were now glued to whatever was happening on the TV screen.

"Be right back," Elena said, already two feet out the door. She locked herself in the bathroom and opened the Stash Grab app to check her messages. There was one, and only one, from Stashiuk4Prez. Scoffing, she clicked on the text. It said, "Will you go to the Valentine's dance with me?"

Elena's jaw dropped. She found herself glancing around the bathroom, looking for a hidden camera or something. There was nothing real about this moment. It had to be a joke. It had to be the universe playing some hilarious prank on her. He, Oliver Prince, just asked her, Elena Chestnut, to a dance. Not just any dance, a Valentine's dance.

And he had no idea. He had no freaking clue what he'd just done.

Grinning hard and leaning into her role as evil witch, Elena composed a response: "Yes! But let's meet there. I'll be wearing a yellow dress."

It was the perfect plan. She'd bought a yellow dress months ago for homecoming, which she'd ended up not attending. Now Oliver would show up at the Valentine's dance, see her wearing yellow, and he'd realize it was her he'd been talking to this whole time—the girl whose family business he was gleefully watching go under, the girl whose presence he could barely endure while she was trying to teach him Latin.

Since Elena was alone in the bathroom and therefore had no one with whom to celebrate her having upper hand, she high fived her own reflection in the mirror over the sink.

• • •

"I mean, you're not wrong. The dancing is amazing."

Harper, sitting crisscross applesauce on the floor in her basement with her back up against the couch, swung her head around to see Oliver, who was lying across the sofa. "Right? The perfect way to spend a lazy Sunday afternoon."

He sat up and swung his legs next to Harper. "I wasn't sure how I'd feel watching *Magic Mike XXL*, but I will be able to walk away from this experience secure in my own heterosexuality and with a healthy appreciation for the male form and all its physical potential."

Harper scrunched up her nose. "See, that's where we're different. Or maybe that's where we're the same. I figured I'd walk away from this movie wanting Channing Tatum to grind against me like I'm one of his welding tools, but instead I'm like, 'Yay guys, you have very good moves, but I'd like to suck face with Amber Heard.'"

"Well, I'm more of a Jada Pinkett-Smith man," Oliver admitted.

"And this is why we're such good friends. We'll never go after the same girl."

"Especially not if the girl you're after is my sister." Oliver winced as Harper tossed a pillow at him.

She took the spot next to Oliver on the couch, dragging her knees up to her chest. "I think I'm actually gay," she said.

Oliver grabbed the remote and shut off the TV.

"I've been walking around for weeks with this whole new

perspective, like the blinders are off my eyes and everything is in HD. For my whole life, I liked guys because it was expected, you know? I, without anyone telling me to, sort of settled into this heteronormative mythology about myself."

"You were straight because you believed you were supposed to be straight."

"It's kind of silly, right?" Harper smiled and patted Oliver's knee. "My brother Matthew is gay. I mean, he's freaking marrying Hakeem this summer. And I've been living a lie my entire life."

"I'm pretty sure figuring out you like girls when you're seventeen doesn't count as living a lie your entire life. You've got quite a few years ahead of you, Harper."

Harper's phone buzzed, and she waved it in Oliver's face after checking the message. "Elena's here." She dictated a text as she typed it. "Come in."

Oliver groaned. It was Sunday afternoon, and he was due for another study session with Elena. They had agreed to meet on neutral ground, Harper's house, with her playing mediator.

Harper peeked at the stairs. "I came out to Elena," she whispered, eyes back on Oliver.

"And she shunned you? She told you she didn't support your lifestyle?" He'd believe absolutely any negative news about Elena Chestnut at this point.

Harper tossed a pillow at him. "No. She was very cool about it, as I knew she would be."

"Please."

"I mean it," Harper said. "She is a lovely person and—" Harper jumped off the couch and ran to the stairs. "She's here!" Harper wrapped Elena in a huge hug, though Elena's arms remained down at her sides as she fixed her scowl on Oliver.

He rolled his eyes, like, what? Was he supposed to be

scared? Hurt? Contrite? She had no power over him.

Wordlessly, Oliver and Elena set up shop at the bar on the far side of the basement, while Harper cued up another movie—this time *Pitch Perfect 2*. "Is this gonna bother you?" Harper shouted as the music of the Barden Bellas filled the entire room.

"I'm fine," Oliver said through gritted teeth.

"Me, too." Elena still glared at Oliver. He got the sense that she was trying to stare him down, to exert dominance over him, like he was a dog she was trying to tame or something. Well, two could play at that game.

Hard eyes fixed on hers, Oliver pulled his Latin book from his bag and plopped it on the bar. "I did my homework," he said.

"Good." Lips pursed, Elena pulled a sheet of folded notebook paper from his book. She opened it, smoothed it out, and started correcting his mistakes with a red pen. In five minutes flat, his homework was a mess of scarlet scribbles.

She laid the paper in front of him and pointed out each mistake. "Here the verb is subjunctive. In this sentence, you want to translate this word as the direct object and this one as the indirect object. I'm almost positive you have no idea what the word *propter* means because you translate it incorrectly every single time—" She paused and spun around on her bar stool as Harper rose from her spot on the couch and marched up the stairs.

"Popcorn!" she announced, halfway up.

Oliver snatched his homework back. "You know, maybe if you'd explain shit instead of just berating me when I get the answer wrong, I might actually learn something."

"Where's the fun in that?" Elena said.

Oliver shoved his book and homework into his bag and hopped off the chair. He had better things to do with his time. "I'm done with this. I'll fail Latin or I'll figure out a way to drop the class, I don't care. Even getting my computer back isn't worth this abuse."

"Abuse?" she said. "You're feeling abused? You're the one who showed up at my event on Friday and ruined my entire night."

"Whatever, Elena, my telling you about our parents was no big deal. You said yourself you already knew about your mom and my dad. Unless you were *lying* about that." He cocked his jaw as she squirmed under his gaze. "And besides, I was trying to be a good guy by telling you."

"If that's your attempt at being a decent person, good luck ever getting anyone to like you." She folded her arms.

"Tell Harper I said good-bye. Oh, and *propter* means 'on account of.'"

"Well, then translate it that way next time!" Elena shouted after him.

Home wasn't any better. As soon as he stepped through the front door, his parents and sister greeted him from the living room. They were seated in a triangle of sorts—Dad and Regina perched on matching loveseats right across from each other, with Mom in a wingback chair between them. A cloud of gloom hung over all three of them.

"Oliver, good," his mom said, clasping her hands in front of her. "We need to talk."

He fixed his eyes on Regina, wishing they had the kind of telepathic magic other twins had. The only sense he got from her furrowed brow was that whatever his mom was about to say, it wasn't good. He plunked himself next to his sister and folded his hands in his lap.

"It's no secret your dad and I have had our issues as of late," she said. "My staying in Florida for the past few months has been a trial separation of sorts." She glanced at Trip, whose gaze was fixed on a water stain in the middle of the coffee table. "Your dad and I, we've decided it's best if we divorce."

Regina's body tensed. "What?"

Their mom's face was soft. "You know we haven't been happy, honey."

Oliver said nothing, even though his mom was right. She and Trip never fought much in front of the kids, but awkward silences, annoyed grumbling, and angry whispers filled most of their time together.

"You can work through this," said Regina. "Go to counseling."

"We've done that," said their mom. "Of course we've done that. We've done all we can do." She reached for Regina's hand, but Regina scooted closer to Oliver, like he was her security blanket.

The close proximity of his sister took Oliver back to Florida. The weekends there had been torture. That's when Regina and Oliver banded together to hide from the bickering, tension, and uncomfortable quiet that loomed over the forty-eight hours when their parents were forced to be in the same house each week. Oliver and Regina had spent every Saturday and Sunday completely on edge, tiptoeing around the undercurrent of stress that permeated their home. The twins used to hide in each other's rooms, distracting themselves with computer games and other such nonsense, waiting for Monday to roll around. Maybe that's why he and his sister were out of synch in North Pole. They hadn't needed to rely on each other as much since the family moved here.

"You haven't even tried living here," said Regina. "You've been in Florida this whole time."

"Honey, the fact that your dad and I are happier apart, doesn't that say something?"

"Dad's not happy," snapped Regina. "Look at him." She gestured toward her father, who was sitting on the other side of the coffee table. "All he does here is work and mope—"

"Your mother's right, Regina," whispered Trip. "This is

for the best." His red eyes suggested otherwise.

Regina shifted her raging gaze to Oliver. "What do you have to say about this?"

"I don't know," he said, still watching his dad, who was gray-faced and shell-shocked. "I mean, where will we live?" Dealing with logistics was way easier than working through emotions.

His mom said, "That hasn't been decided yet, but I suppose you can stay here or move back to Florida, whichever you choose. We want to make this easy on you. That's the most important thing to both your dad and me."

"You want to make this easy on us? Too late for that." Regina jumped up and glared at Oliver, like all of this was his fault. "Why aren't you more angry or sad or something, you robot?"

He frowned. Regina always burned hotter than he did emotionally, but directing her furor his way was unfair. "I'm in shock."

"Well, snap out of it." She literally snapped in front of his face, and he brushed her hand aside. "This is really happening. Our parents are splitting up. They're tearing our family apart."

"We've been apart, Regina," said their mom. "Not much is going to change—"

"Everything is going to change." Tears streamed down Regina's face.

This hubbub and all its raw emotion were too much for Oliver. He latched onto one tiny glimmer of hope in this gigantic mess of garbage. "Can I have my computer back?" he asked. Maybe his mom was feeling so guilty at this point, she'd give him anything he wanted.

"Are you kidding me right now?" Regina said.

His mom frowned. "I don't think so, honey," she said. "Your grades have improved and your dad says you've been doing better socially without it. I think we should keep this little no-electronics experiment clipping along."

A cold sweat creeping down his back, Oliver rose.

"Oh, now you've finally pissed him off," Regina said, folding her arms across her chest. "Poor Oliver can't have his computer back. It's the only stinking thing he cares about."

"Are we done here?" he asked, eyes locked on his mom. He removed all emotion from his voice. Sure, he was angry and frustrated and sad, but Regina couldn't know that. Not after her robot comment.

"I suppose so," said his mother.

Oliver marched up to his room and shut the door, slowly, quietly. He left the lights off and listened to the hum of nothing in his room. The silence threatened to strangle him. A knot in his throat, he opened up his Stash Grab app and messaged the only person he could talk to, proud_hoser. "My parents are getting a divorce."

Chapter Ten

Elena sat down to watch *Pitch Perfect 2* with Harper after Oliver left.

"I don't see why you two can't be civil to each other," Harper said, her mouth full of popcorn. "I mean, it's not like you have to pledge your undying love or propose marriage or anything, just treat each other like human beings."

"I hope you'll tell him this, too," said Elena.

"I will and I do," Harper insisted.

"Because I'm not the only jerk here."

Harper patted her on the leg. "You're not the only jerk." She raised her eyebrows, and Elena understood the silent "But you are a jerk," in that statement.

That was Elena's cue to leave. She pulled on her running shoes. "I'd better get going before it gets dark." Her mom had dropped her off at Harper's, but Elena had wanted to run home. It was a good seven miles from Harper's house in the golf resort to Elena's place in town.

Harper waved good-bye, her focus now on a fictional life-or-death *a capella* tournament.

Elena's friends and family always made fun of her for running outside in the dead of winter, but Elena loved it. This was the best time for an outdoor run. The cold air slapped the life into her, gave her clarity. She dashed out Harper's front entrance, ran past the abandoned log cabin next door, and kept going and going and going until her phone buzzed. Elena slowed to a stop. There was a Stash nearby.

She grinned. This was true contentment: a life-affirming run and the Stash Grab competition, where she was currently sitting in the top five. Elena was so close to winning the plane tickets that she could almost feel a sandy beach between her toes. She clicked on the tiny virtual Stash, and the question popped up: Stan Stashiuk has a birthmark on his back. Which state does it resemble?

Elena grinned. She knew this one. It was basic Stash trivia. His birthmark was shaped like Illinois.

She typed the answer, and Elena's mood brightened even more as the little Stash disappeared behind her avatar at the bottom of the screen. This game was kind of stupid, but she loved the rush that accompanied her success. Stash Grab was something she had control over, something she was good at. It gave her purpose, too. She wanted to win. She wanted to go on spring break with Harper. She was tired of missing out.

She took off running again, using the abandoned golf cart paths as her running track. When she was nearly to the entrance of the resort, her phone buzzed again, and once more she slowed to a halt.

This time there wasn't a Stash in the area. It was a message from Stashiuk4Prez. Elena's cheeks flushed. How dare he interrupt her run? Her finger hovered over the delete button, about to erase her entire conversation with Stashiuk4Prez, AKA Oliver Prince, but curiosity got the best of her. Biting her lip and grumbling at her own weakness, she clicked on the text.

"My parents are getting a divorce," it said.

Numb, Elena slowly lowered the phone back into her pocket. She should ignore this. She should butt out and not get involved. He'd sent this to proud_hoser, not to her. This message was not meant for Elena Chestnut's eyes.

But, she thought, as she exited the resort and ran down Holly Road to her house, Oliver was reaching out to this specific girl for support. His life was already pretty shitty at this point, and how much deeper would it sink his mood if the girl he liked completely ignored his very important, very personal message?

This was an opportunity for Elena to practice civility. This was her chance to prove she wasn't the evilest witch in town.

She paused on the corner of Holly and Spruce and wrote him back, "That completely sucks. I'm so sorry."

"Thanks," he said. "You're the first person I told. It feels more real all of a sudden. My mom and dad are splitting up."

Elena's heart beat faster, a lump in her throat. If his mom and dad were divorcing, what did that mean for her own parents? What if Oliver had been right? What if her mom and his dad were having an affair? With shaking hands, she asked, "Do you know why this is happening?"

He said, "It's not a shock or anything. They've been unhappy for a long time. It's just...a lot of emotions right now."

A touch of relief entered Elena's body, which was then replaced by guilt. She shouldn't feel happy that his situation had nothing to do with her mom and dad. She told him, "You know you can talk to me," and, oddly, she meant it.

He said, "It's a mix of things, you know? I'm sitting here alone in my room and I'm sad and hurt, but also relieved. And then I feel guilty for the relief."

"Why do you feel guilty?" Instead of turning toward home, Elena hung a right on Spruce and headed into town.

If she was going to have this conversation, she might as well catch some Stashes in the meantime.

"My mom said I can stay here in North Pole with my dad, if I want. I guess I feel guilty because I'm glad. I don't want to leave."

Before she'd known that Oliver Prince was the one on the other end of this dialogue, Elena would've said something like, "I don't want you to leave." Now she said, "It's good they're letting you make your own choices."

He didn't write back immediately, and Elena figured he was probably trying to decipher her message and its lack of lovey-dovey treacle. When he finally responded, he said, "Let's talk about something else. What are you doing?"

"I'm in town catching Stashes," she said, though she regretted it right away. What if he came out looking for her? She sighed. Oh, well. Then the cat would be out of the bag. "I just caught a hundred pointer outside Joyeaux Noel."

"What was the question?" he asked.

"Something about Dolores Page's kids who are all named after reindeer," she told him.

"Have fun," he said.

Elena kept going, running up and down the streets of North Pole, hurtling over snowdrifts, galumphing through the sludge. When she was out in front of Danny Garland's house, catching a Stash about his neighbor's cat, she got another message from Stashiuk4Prez.

"There's a two-hundred point Stash in the park."

Elena froze. What did this mean? Was he waiting for her at the park? Was this his way of forcing a meet-up? Elena glanced around. She was just down the road from the park. Was Oliver Prince there waiting for proud_hoser? And how would he feel if Elena showed up instead? How would he feel if no one came?

Shaking from guilt, Elena ambled toward the park. What

should she do? Should she reveal herself or not? Her goal had been to use the two-block walk as a chance to make up her mind, but her decision was no clearer by the time she reached the playground.

Hiding behind a tree, Elena's eyes swung to each corner of the park. The place was deserted, an empty plot of land covered by a vast blanket of snow. She detected no sign of Oliver or anyone else. Elena stepped out from her hiding spot and tiptoed toward the playground, feeling exposed as she crept out into the open. That's when the Stash popped up. Elena's eyes swept the area again. Still no sign of Oliver. She read the question.

"What is Sam Anderson's favorite movie?"

Elena laughed. This was a question tailor made for her. Except, did they want to know the movie he always said was his favorite movie (*A Few Good Men*), or did they want to know his actual favorite movie? She went for the latter. "*Mission: Impossible III.*"

The Stash disappeared behind her avatar.

She hesitated for a second, sensing hidden eyes watching her every move, then she messaged Oliver. "Thanks. I caught one by Danny's house, if you're looking."

"I am," he said. "There's one in the deli section at the grocery store, but you'd better hurry. Ludlum's is closing soon."

Relief flooded her system. He wasn't trying to meet her. He was simply trying to help the girl he liked win Stash Grab.

Grinning like a fool, she took off toward Evergreen Street and the grocery store. She got to the deli just in time, and she caught the Stash, despite stern frowns of disapproval from the owner, Bob Ludlum, who was angry at her for not buying anything.

"Yeah, Bob," she shouted on her way out, "like you've never 'just browsed' at Chestnut's!"

She caught another Stash in the arcade and another outside the gun shop. Adrenaline coursed through her body. She had reached the point of invincibility. She hadn't felt this good in weeks, maybe months. She messaged Stashiuk4Prez, forgetting momentarily that he and Oliver Prince were the same person. "There are a million Stashes out tonight. We are kicking so much ass!"

As Elena jogged down Main Street, she waved to her fellow North Pole residents. Sam and his buddies hovered outside the video store. An elderly pair—was that Frank and Dolores Page?—kissed in the moonlight under a streetlamp. As her curfew, ten thirty, approached, Elena checked her spot on the Stash Grab leader board. She was near the top— number three. Then she skidded around the corner by the bakery and nearly tripped over her own boot when she saw Oliver Prince hovering outside the Chinese restaurant, which was rebelliously called "The Chinese Restaurant" and not something Christmasy, like "Away in Lo Mein-ger."

He had his phone out as well. The two of them stared at each other for a beat, then Elena glanced down as her phone buzzed. "Tonight was exactly the distraction I needed. Thank you."

She looked up, but Oliver Prince was gone.

Elena trudged home. Did he know? Was that last message his way of saying "I see you?" That couldn't be it. How would he know? Why would he even suspect? She chuckled to herself. She'd been completely nice and civil to him all evening. That was not on-brand for Elena Chestnut.

At home, Elena found her parents in the living room, sitting next to each other on the couch, a foot of space between them. They weren't watching TV; they were staring at the door, like they were waiting for Elena to come home. The scene took her breath away, and the word "divorce" pounded in her head.

Elena took her time pulling off her boots in the hallway. When she stepped into the living room, her mom and dad straightened up, all business. "Elena, we want to be honest with you." There was a sharpness to her mom's voice.

Her mom pointed to the chair across from them, but Elena didn't take it. She stayed where she was, gloves in hand, and folded her arms across her chest.

"Honey," her dad said, "the business isn't doing well."

Elena resisted a, "Well, duh."

Her mom drew in a deep breath. "We've been having trouble paying our bills."

"That's why we went to Wisconsin to see your aunt," her dad said. It sounded like they were reciting lines from a play. Elena wouldn't have been surprised to learn they'd been practicing this since she left for Harper's house that afternoon.

"We asked to borrow money but she said no." Elena's mom frowned. "She said the business was going to go under no matter what we did."

Elena exhaled. At least they were starting to be honest with her. That was progress. And at least they weren't talking about splitting up. "What about the money from Friday night?" When they'd arrived home from Aunt Patti's earlier this morning, Elena had been so excited to tell them about the big night at Chestnut's after the Stash Grab Dash. They hadn't seemed super jazzed then, and they didn't now.

"It's not enough," said her dad.

"One good night isn't going to save the store." Her mom glowered at him.

"But it helps," Elena said. "And doesn't it prove that we can survive if we try doing some new things once in a while? People loved the event."

"Trying new things." Her mom cleared her throat.

Ignoring his wife, her dad said, "They loved it this one time. We can't do special events every week. People wouldn't come."

"So, what now?" said Elena. Panic settled into her bones and cold crept up her limbs. What did any of this mean?

"Patti gave me and your mom a loan to get us back on our feet." Her dad reached over to grab his wife's knee, but she scooted away. "We're going to get new jobs. We're going to start over."

"Maybe even in a new town," her mom said with a hint of scorn.

"We've been here for so long." Her dad shot his wife a warning glance.

"Are we moving?" Elena said through clenched teeth. Here they were again, making decisions without including her.

"Nothing's been decided yet, honey."

"We've been running the store for twenty years," her dad said. "We never got to take vacations or even go away for a weekend. We've been chained to that place. We're kind of looking forward to exploring new options."

"You are," her mom muttered.

Her dad ignored this. "Your aunt has a job for me at her company in Wisconsin."

Elena knew her dad was trying to make her feel better, to turn this whole situation into a positive, but she was nowhere near ready for that. They were screwing her. She was the one who'd tried to keep the store going, to bring in new business. She was the one who had to give up her school trip and quit the track team. She was the one who was going to have to take out a billion-dollar loan to pay for college and who might have to leave her school before her senior year.

Her dad grinned like this was the greatest news in the history of the world. "This is such a fantastic opportunity for us. It's an adventure."

"Yeah. An adventure." An adventure Elena had no

desire to embark upon. She held up her phone. "I've gotta call Harper." She dashed up to her room, taking the stairs two at a time.

When she was alone in her room, however, she didn't call Harper. It wasn't that Harper wouldn't understand, but…no. That was kind of it. Harper's family was loaded. She couldn't fathom worrying about money or her dad's business closing or any of that. In Harper's world, everything was always okay, even when it wasn't. Things unfailingly worked out in the end. Elena didn't need sunshine right now.

She opened up her Stash Grab app and messaged the one person in her life she could talk to freely right now. She wrote Stashiuk4Prez. "My parents are selling their business, and I probably have to move to Wisconsin."

"Shit," he wrote back right away.

"Yeah. We're both having a pretty bad night, aren't we?" Tears stung Elena's eyes.

"Messaging you has made it a bit less terrible," he responded.

A tear rolled down Elena's cheek. Chatting with her enemy was exactly what she needed right now. Only Oliver understood what she was going through at the moment—his parents were messing up his life as much as Elena's were screwing with hers. "You know what?" she told him. "You're right."

. . .

Oliver messaged proud_hoser once more on his walk home from school Tuesday afternoon. "I will try watching *Gilmore Girls*, but no promises."

"You're gonna love it, don't worry," she replied, with a winky-face.

Ever since they'd opened up about their respective family

problems, Oliver and proud_hoser had been messaging each other with more urgency and more frequency. They were on borrowed time now. His family was in flux; hers was about to move out of state.

"And you have to promise me you'll check out *Black Mirror*," he said.

"It's a deal."

He hesitated a moment, then wrote, "And maybe, after the dance on Friday, we can watch this stuff together some time." The fact that the two of them had plans to meet at the Valentine's dance this week was one topic they avoided. Oliver wasn't sure why proud_hoser never brought it up, but he felt superstitious discussing the whole thing. Like, if he mentioned the dance, maybe she'd take that as her cue to back out. It didn't seem too implausible. Oliver was already up half the night worried about meeting her, worried about all the potential disasters that could destroy their fragile relationship, or whatever this was.

His most potent nightmare: that Regina and proud_hoser were the same person, and she had fabricated this entire identity for the sole purpose of messing with Oliver.

In response to his suggestion that they Netflix and chill together sometime, proud_hoser sent him a smiley face, which Oliver took at face value.

He'd spent the past two days at school trying to figure out who might be behind the proud_hoser account. The biggest clue he had so far was that her family owned a business in town, one they were about to sell. There was Dottie, whose family owned the bakery. Gretchen Ludlum's dad owned the grocery store. Katie Murphy's parents owned the gun shop.

And, of course, there was Elena Chestnut.

But Oliver banished that unpleasant notion to the outer fringes of his mind.

When Oliver got home, he discovered his dad curled up

on one of the loveseats in the living room, sleeping in the middle of the afternoon, with a fire blazing in the hearth. Almost an entire ream of paper and several empty cans of Michelob Golden Lite were strewn across the table in front of him. Oliver recycled the cans. His dad wasn't usually a big drinker, especially not alone during the day.

With a knotted stomach, Oliver started stacking the papers, figuring they were divorce papers for his dad to sign. But the header on page one caught his eye.

It said "Plan for Prince's and Chestnut's," and there was a neon pink Post-It in the top right corner. "Please read this, Trip," the note begged. "I think my idea could really work. If you get on board, then we only need to convince Tom. Ha-ha. Sincerely, Emily."

Emily. Emily Chestnut, the woman who used to be engaged to Oliver's father.

But this wasn't a romantic proposition. It was all business.

Standing there in the living room, Oliver read through Mrs. Chestnut's plan. The idea was an interesting one—a collaboration between the two stores, but with a hint of independence built in. Chestnut's would carry the fall and winter sports in their store, Prince's would take care of spring and summer. They'd work as a team—sharing customers, profits, and employees. It'd solve the problem of both shops being too small to handle the inventory. She suggested bringing the stores into the new century with a website capable of handling sales. Oliver started developing the site in his head. The one Prince's had now was from ten years ago, when someone forced his grandfather to buy a domain, and it was basically just a parking lot.

Mrs. Chestnut painted a picture of what it would be like— Chestnut's would be busy in the winter, while Prince's would thrive in the summer. They could host events with athletes and do demonstrations—how to tie survival knots, how to care for your snowboard, how to properly chip out of a sand trap. As she pointed out in her plan, part of the problem with the non-specialty megastores like Wal-Mart was the lack of expertise available in shop. Prince's and Chestnut's, with the help of some of the more athletically inclined townies, could provide that level of help and know-how.

"What are you doing?" Oliver's dad barked.

Oliver hid the papers behind his back and faced his father, who was now upright and rubbing his temples. "Cleaning up."

Trip held out a hand. "Give me that."

Oliver shrugged, but held onto the stack. "It's an interesting idea. We've been fighting Chestnut's for so long, competing for the same customers. Maybe teaming up isn't the worst idea." He remembered the photos of his dad and Mr. Chestnut in the album inside Prince's office. They had been friends since childhood. Emily Chestnut was set on rekindling that friendship and helping both stores, not seducing Oliver's dad. "It's not like Prince's has been doing that well."

"It's moot," said Trip, standing and beckoning again for the papers. "I'm closing the store."

"What? What do you mean 'closing the store'? What would you do instead?" With the money his dad had made from selling the restaurants down in Florida, he could do whatever he wanted. He could open a new restaurant here. He could become a ski bum.

"I've been thinking." Trip paced in front of the fireplace. "Maybe the problem is North Pole. Maybe it was a mistake to move here."

"No," Oliver said right away. "It wasn't a mistake. It's been great, actually. Regina and I have made new friends. We like it here." proud_hoser was here.

Trip laughed. "Your mom wants a divorce. The business isn't doing so great. We're stuck in an icy tundra. Mistake, mistake, mistake."

Oliver couldn't argue with that last point about the cold. "But you always wanted to take over your dad's store. It was your dream. You had to go after your dream."

"Yeah, but that's not going well, is it? You've been working there. You see how slow it's been."

"It's February. It'll pick up as the weather gets warmer." It was the ebb and flow of life in North Pole. They were in the lull right now, the dead of winter, before spring and the summer vacationers. "People hibernate this time of year."

"Maybe," said his dad. "But they're still running around playing your game. They're just not coming into the store to buy stuff."

"They will," said Oliver. He shook the papers in front of his dad's face. North Pole was much closer to Wisconsin than Florida was. Oliver was not going to move back to the southeastern tip of the country now, not when things were just starting to heat up between him and proud_hoser. He was even willing to team up with Elena Chestnut and her family. These were desperate times. "And this could be the solution."

"I failed." Trip picked up an empty beer can Oliver had missed and tilted it toward his mouth. A few drops dribbled past his lips. "I ruined the business my family spent decades building. I never saw this coming. I've never failed at anything."

"You still haven't," Oliver said.

"And your mom…we were doing so well before this whole Minnesota thing."

"No, you weren't," said Oliver. He clenched his fists, incredulous that he was about to insert himself into someone else's business, but his dad was not thinking straight. "The divorce is a positive thing, Dad. For everyone. Maybe I'm a pragmatic, unfeeling robot for seeing that, but it's true."

"I'm going to close the store," his dad announced.

"No, Dad. Don't make any rash—"

"It's for the good of the family and the good of the town.

I'm going to bow out, let the Chestnuts have a monopoly on sporting goods in North Pole. If Emily wants it, she can have it."

"But what does that mean for—"

"We're going to move back to Florida to be a family again," said Trip, standing up. "It's the right thing to do." He snatched Mrs. Chestnut's papers from Oliver's clutches and tossed them into the fire. Oliver stood rooted to the floor and watched his future in North Pole burn.

Chapter Eleven

"You guys, you guys, you guys! We are in the home stretch of Stash Grab, and you're sitting here in Santabucks studying Latin!" Harper danced around the table where Elena and Oliver were trying to study.

"He has a big test on Friday," said Elena. "I need to help him pass it." Elena shot him a quick smile and focused on Harper again. This was their first study session since Oliver had stormed out of Harper's basement on Sunday. Elena thanked the universe for Harper's presence, because her mind and body were a clutter of confusion. She had just spent the past three days messaging Stashiuk4Prez more than ever and about increasingly personal stuff, knowing the whole time that the guy on the other end was Oliver Prince. And the thought, amazingly, no longer completely bummed her out.

Elena had been a bundle of nerves on Monday morning, and she couldn't for the life of her figure out why. She didn't have any tests or quizzes scheduled. When she took her seat in social studies for first period, she opened up her assignment notebook and checked to make sure she hadn't forgotten about a paper or anything. She hadn't.

Then, right before the bell rang, the door opened and in walked Oliver Prince with his floppy auburn hair and his warm brown eyes, and Elena's cheeks began to ache. She touched her face. She was smiling. At Oliver Prince. Her stomach was effervescing. Because of Oliver Prince.

He, Oliver Prince as Stashiuk4Prez, had chatted with her until midnight on Sunday, talking first about their parents' situations, and then about other personal stuff. He told her he had a sister he wished he understood better. She told him she wished she had any siblings at all. He confessed that he was so shy he hadn't really dated anyone before. She told him that her romantic experience was limited to an unfortunate few-week dalliance with one of North Pole's biggest dumbasses.

"Kevin Snow?" he'd asked right away.

She'd laughed then, and she laughed now, in Santabucks, with Oliver Prince sitting right across from her. Elena clamped her mouth shut immediately.

He frowned, bewilderment settling into his warm, suddenly delicious brown eyes. How could she have ever convinced herself he was a six? He was a nine. He never wasn't a nine.

"Sorry. Just remembered something funny." She shook herself out of her stupor. It was foolish to think this way. He was still Oliver Prince. That hadn't changed, and was never going to change. Whatever existed between them, online or elsewhere, was dead on arrival. Elena sucked in her cheeks to temper the perma-grin she'd been wearing since Monday morning. "We're here to study, Harper," she said, tapping her pencil eraser on the table.

Harper flailed her arm toward the window. "Look outside! Everyone is catching Stashes!"

Elena followed her friend's gesture. Harper was right. The sun had been out all day, the snow was starting to melt just a hint, and throngs of people scurried up and down Main Street with their eyes on their phones, trying to maximize productivity during this unseasonable warm spell. Channeling her mother, Elena wondered how no one had managed to seriously injure themselves yet. Elena turned to Harper. "You don't even care if you win."

"I do!" said Harper. "I always care about winning!"

Elena couldn't argue with that. "Harper is a chronic winner."

"You're not as big a winner as my brother Danny," Brian Garland added from behind the counter.

Harper rolled her eyes. "Please."

Slowly, cautiously, Elena swung her gaze to Oliver. "What do you say?" she asked. "Are you good? Is there anything else you'd like to go over?" She glanced down at her own notes and shuffled through her papers to see if they'd missed anything important. She peeked up at him. "Did you hear me? Do you want me to go over anything else?"

"You're not yelling at me," said Oliver.

"Do you want me to?" She felt her eyes sparkle.

"I'm just…" He pinched his arm. "No, I'm awake."

Elena raised her brows. "I'm taking my job seriously," she said. "You trust me with your Latin grade—"

"My mom does," he said. "And she said I need to keep meeting with you if I ever want to see my computer again."

"Either way," said Elena. "I…am here for you."

Oliver scrunched up his nose, then rotated slowly away from this new Bizarro World version of Elena and focused on Harper. "You guys go have fun," he said.

"Okay." Harper grabbed Elena's arm.

"Come with us," Elena blurted.

Oliver paused, having only gotten one arm through his jacket.

"Or whatever…" Elena shrugged, shaking her head. "Do

what you want."

Harper clutched Oliver's arm and yanked him toward the door. "Yeah, come with us! It'll be fun, and you probably know all the answers."

"You know I don't," he said.

"Please, your sister can't keep a secret."

His eyes twinkled at Harper. "She can about this." Oliver nodded toward Elena. "You're playing?"

She blushed. "Yes." Then reluctantly, "Your game is fun, Oliver, and I want to win it."

He grinned. "Cool."

The three of them shoved on their coats, hats, and mittens and ran out onto the street with their phones at the ready, dodging other Stash Grabbers who were doing the same thing. They caught Stash after Stash, running all over the place—from the park up to the edge of the golf resort where Harper lived, and over by Mags's restaurant on the far west side of town.

In front of the diner, Harper bent forward and rested her hands on her knees, panting. "When did you start running, Oliver? You're almost as bad as her." She jabbed a finger toward Elena.

Oliver grinned. "Something I just took up recently."

Elena's heart pounded as she focused hard on Harper. He had started running because of her, though he had no idea that it was because of her. In fact, he'd probably shit several bricks if he ever found out. This whole situation was so weird and surreal. "You want to rest, Harper?"

She shook her head. "I can keep up with you two."

"I'm just saying," said Elena, "it's"—she checked her phone—"five thirty. We can stop for a bite—"

Harper waved her off. "I'm fine, I said." She straightened up, waving her phone in the air. "In fact, I'm better than fine. I'm going to catch that Stash over by the video store before you do!"

Elena and Oliver jogged after Harper as she sprinted down Cedar Street, toward Main. And then they paused and watched—in slow motion—as Harper bolted across the street, hit a patch of black ice, flew into the air, and landed hard on her right leg.

"Holy crap, Harper!" Elena darted into the street toward her friend, barely checking for cars.

Harper's brother, Sam, who was working at the video store, ran out right away. He got to Harper at about the same time Elena and Oliver did. The two guys wrapped Harper's arms around their shoulders and dragged her to the safety of the sidewalk, while Elena salvaged her phone and wiped slush off the screen. She dashed toward Harper and surveyed the damage. "Are you okay? Did you hit your head?" Elena held up a hand. "How many fingers am I holding up?"

"Elena, you're wearing mittens."

"Very good," Elena said. "You passed the test."

"Is my phone okay?" Harper reached for it, and Elena handed it to her. When the screen glowed to life, Harper sighed in relief.

"Are you sure you're okay?" asked Sam.

"I'm fine. Totally fine." Harper pushed the boys away and tried to stand. Her right ankle crumbled beneath her weight.

Elena gasped. "Should we call 911?"

"No." Sam ducked under her arm and helped his sister take the pressure off her leg. He glanced around. "She just needs to go to urgent care."

"I do not," said Harper.

"You really, really do," Elena said.

Sam nodded toward the video store. "I've gotta close up. Maurice won't be back for an hour or so."

"I'll take her." Oliver reached for Harper. She pushed him away, while still trying to open her Stash Grab app.

"I'll go with," Elena said.

Sam shook his head. "I'll take her. She's my clumsy sister."

"Yeah, and you're a graceful swan," Harper said, scrolling through the apps on her phone.

"If you want to take her, Sam, I can watch the store for you," Elena said. "It's dead in there anyway."

Sam grinned, nudging Oliver in the side. "Everybody's out and about playing Stash Grab. The town is of a singular mindset. You did that, man." Sam nodded toward the door. "You don't mind?" he asked Elena.

"Not at all." She couldn't stop staring at her friend's leg. Her booted right foot dangled limply beneath her knee.

Sam tried to guide Harper toward his car, but she rooted herself to the ground with her one good leg.

"But Stash Grab," she whined.

"You're done," said Elena. "Go get your ankle fixed. Please. For the love of all that is good and pure."

Harper pouted, while she simultaneously winced in pain.

"She really needs to go now," Elena said.

Oliver held out his hand. "Give me your phone. I'll hunt Stashes for you."

"That's cheating," said Sam.

"He doesn't know any of the answers," said Elena. "I can vouch for that."

Oliver waved dismissively at Harper. "And she's not going to win anyway."

"Yes, I am." Harper straightened up.

Elena patted her head. "You keep telling yourself that. You're, like, fifteenth on the leader board. The truth hurts sometimes." She put her hands on her friend's shoulders, then pulled her in for a big hug, careful not to jostle the bad leg. "Go get fixed, damn it."

Elena and Oliver stood on the curb next to each other and watched as Sam helped Harper hop over to the old, rusted out pickup truck that his family had had for years. Convinced her friend was in good hands, Elena sighed. "Well, I'd better go in there and watch another empty store. It's what I'm good at. At least it will distract me from worrying about Harper."

Oliver followed her into the store, and Elena felt nervous all of a sudden, first date nervous. "Don't you have Stashes to catch?" she asked.

"I didn't want to abandon you." He stared out the window and down the road toward the hospital. He spun around. "I hope she's okay."

"I'm sure she will be," said Elena, trying to push the image of her friend's mangled ankle from her mind. "She's a tough broad."

"What do you need help with?" He rubbed his hands together and blew warm air into his hands.

Elena shrugged. "I guess we're supposed to hang out and help anyone who comes in, if anyone comes in." Elena dropped her bag and outerwear onto the floor behind the counter.

"This place is so cool." Oliver glanced around. The video store was like the Beast's library for movie fans. There were shelves and shelves of DVDs and VHS tapes, very old school. Posters from movies ranging from *Citizen Kane* to *Wet Hot American Summer* lined the walls. He stopped in the horror movie section and checked out a DVD copy of *Susperia*. "It's amazing they stay in business."

"A lot of tourists rent movies here, because, I don't know if you've noticed, but there's not a lot to do at night in North Pole."

"Especially not in the winter." Oliver glanced up at her.

"Right," she agreed. "Also, this is the only movie theater in town, and they're always doing events, like they've got a rom-com marathon coming up this Friday for people who aren't going to the dance." She coughed. Oh my God, she just said "dance." "And of course there's the Saturday night classic movie show. Have you ever gone to one of those?"

Oliver shook his head.

"It's a lot of fun. It's, like, the thing to do if you've got nothing going on. Maurice charges five bucks a person, and you get a pop and a bag of popcorn." She stepped around the counter and walked toward the back of the store, where she opened a door and flipped on the light switch. "See?"

Oliver came over and checked out the room, which was a little screening space filled with couches, beanbags, and other comfy chairs. A large projection screen took up one whole wall. This was also one of the best make out spots in town. She'd spent a few evenings with Kevin Snow on those beanbags last year. Barf.

"Do you realize"—Oliver leaned against the doorjamb across from her—"we have not fought once all day."

"Don't ruin it." Elena folded her arms and pressed her lips together, trying to hold back a grin.

"I don't want to ruin it. It's nice." He nodded around the store. "I like it here."

"In the video store?" she asked.

"In North Pole." His eyes grew stormy. "I'm moving back to Florida."

"What?" she whispered. This was news to her. She'd been going on and on for days about her parents potentially packing the family's bags for Wisconsin, but Stashiuk4Prez had never once mentioned leaving the upper Midwest.

He stared deeply into her eyes, and Elena wondered what he saw now—his mortal enemy, a borderline friend, or the girl he'd been chatting with unknowingly for weeks? Did he somehow know? Did he sense it? "I just found out last night. And"—he ran his fingers through his copper hair—"don't shoot the messenger this time, okay?" He grinned, but Elena's stomach dropped to her ankles. "I don't think our parents are having an affair. Actually, I found this plan your mom had come up with to save the stores—both stores—and I can't stop thinking about it."

"My mom?"

Oliver nodded. "I found my dad on the couch yesterday, drunk and just, ugh, and he had this stack of papers about merging the two stores and sort of, like, sharing the burden. Your store would carry the fall and winter sports equipment. My dad's store would do spring and summer." He paused. "I thought it was a really solid idea, actually."

Elena blinked, waiting for him to go on. She'd spent the last several days sharing confidences with the boy who was supposed to be her archenemy, but this was the strangest conversation she'd had in a while.

"My dad won't go for it. He said we're moving back to Florida, and he wants to work things out with my mom, though I don't see that ending well. And he tossed your mom's idea in the fire. Literally."

Without thinking, Elena reached over, grabbed his hand, and squeezed. To her amazement, he didn't brush her away or recoil in disgust. He squeezed her hand back, then let it go. "We should come here sometime," he said.

Elena's heart pounded. "Yeah," she said.

"I mean with Harper or whoever," he added.

"Of course. With Harper."

As if on cue, Harper's phone buzzed, and Oliver held it up. "I should probably catch her a few Stashes. She'll kill me if she gets back and finds out I've done nothing for her score."

"She literally will," said Elena.

He gripped her hand one more time before waltzing out the front door.

• • •

Replaying the previous scene in his head, Oliver mindlessly caught a few Stashes for Harper as he wandered down Main Street away from the video store. He had just carried on a civil conversation with Elena Chestnut. A very civil conversation. More than civil. He had opened up to her about his family moving back to Florida—something he hadn't told anyone, not even proud_hoser—and she had been very supportive. So supportive, she even touched his hand; and instead of running away screaming, he touched hers back.

Oliver had entered *The Twilight Zone*.

Were he and Elena Chestnut becoming…friends?

He shuddered and checked the Stash Grab app, trying to lose himself in the world of tiny, computer-generated Stan Stashiuks. He had only imagined a connection to Elena. That's all it was. He was sad about leaving North Pole, and he was desperate to latch onto any glimmer of hope. Letting Elena in on their parents' plan to save the stores was that ray of light. He wanted her—needed her—to be his ally in this, and he had projected that role onto her. She wasn't his friend. She had never been his friend. He had no doubt willingly missed a very obvious negative undertone to Elena's words. It was entirely possible she had been making fun of him the entire time, but his brain was too big an emotional mess to detect it.

It was the only rational explanation.

Cold and hungry, he rambled toward Santabucks for sustenance. Brian Garland, Danny's brother, who was working the counter, greeted Oliver. "Back again?"

"My stomach's about to eat itself." Oliver clutched his midsection.

"Did I see you playing Stash Grab?" asked Brian. "Isn't that off-sides? You created the game."

Oliver glanced down at his phone. "I'm helping out Harper. She hurt her leg and refused to go to the hospital because she needed to catch Stashes." Shrugging, Oliver glanced up at Brian. "I told her I'd help her. I don't actually know the answers."

Brian cocked an eyebrow.

"I don't," said Oliver. "My sister wrote the questions and placed the Stashes. Anyway, Harper's so far behind, it doesn't matter."

"True that," agreed Brian. "She's never going to catch Danny. He wins everything, you know."

"I've heard," said Oliver.

"Speaking of Harper." Brian filled a paper cup with hot cocoa. "You were in here with Elena before."

A wave of fatigue washed over Oliver. He'd been trying so hard to evict Elena from his mind, and now here was Brian bringing her up again. The universe hated Oliver. "She's tutoring me."

Brian placed a lid on the cup and handed it to Oliver, who sipped a bit of cocoa that had spilled onto the cover. "Is it true?"

Oliver slipped one of those cardboard sleeves over his cup. "Is what true?"

"Is she moving to Wisconsin?"

Oliver dropped his drink. The contents of the cup splashed against his boots and jeans, scalding his shins.

"Shoot," said Brian, dashing around the counter, wielding a wet rag. "Was it too hot?"

"N-no," stammered Oliver. "It was my fault. I'm clumsy." He crouched down and gathered the empty cup and busted lid while Brian wiped up the hot cocoa. "You said 'Wisconsin'?" he asked.

"Yeah." Brian straightened up, dropped the dirty rag on the counter, and grabbed a mop. "My mom, always the gossip, heard Elena's mom talking to somebody about it."

"Oh," said Oliver. "So, just rumors."

"Well, I don't know. I thought so, but then her dad came in

here the other day and said something about how their store wasn't doing so hot, and maybe it was time for a change."

Bile rose to Oliver's throat.

"It sucks if she is leaving," said Brian, dunking the mop into the pail. "You never want to see the hot girls leave."

"Elena Chestnut?" said Oliver.

Brian laughed, walking back behind the counter. "I should know my audience better. You're Oliver Prince. You probably think she looks like an ogre or something."

"That's exactly what I think," said Oliver.

Brian grabbed a fresh cup and started pouring more hot cocoa.

Oliver waved him off. "Never mind."

"You don't want it?"

Oliver frantically shook his head. "I lost my appetite."

"You sure, man?"

Oliver nodded.

"Sorry." Brian grinned. "Probably all the Elena Chestnut talk."

"That's it."

Numb, Oliver floated out of Santabucks. Back on the sidewalk, he leaned against the outer wall of the café and watched his fellow townsfolk scurry up and down Main Street, catching Stashes, completely unaware that Oliver's entire world had just been upended. He drew in three long, deep breaths, then assessed the information he'd just learned.

Elena's family's business was failing, and they were moving to Wisconsin.

proud_hoser's family's business was closing, and they, too, were moving to Wisconsin.

Coincidence?

Though he hadn't eaten in hours, Oliver's stomach was full of concrete.

Working himself into a fit, he joined the throngs of people

marching along Main Street. Elena had hoodwinked him. She had known the whole time and was playing him for a fool. She despised him, and tricking him into falling for her online persona was her last big *screw you* to Oliver Prince before peacing out to Wisconsin.

Unless it wasn't.

Unless she hadn't known who he was this whole time.

But she had to have known. She had to have been messing with him. That was precisely the kind of thing Elena Chestnut would do. It was the only option that fit the narrative he'd constructed in his head.

Suppressing the acid reflux in his throat, he slid to a halt outside the video store. Elena was still in there, leaning over the counter, reading a magazine. Her long, silky dark brown hair cascaded over one arm like a chocolate waterfall.

As if she knew she was being watched, Elena shook her hair behind her shoulders and stood straight, turning her gaze toward the window. A slow smile engulfed her entire face as she caught sight of Oliver across the street. His renegade facial muscles pulled themselves into a grin, despite his mind's protestations. Elena waved, and Oliver had to physically push his arm down to his side to keep his rogue limb from responding in kind. Then he took off running.

To distract himself once again, Oliver played Stash Grab for Harper—ducking into alleyways and traipsing through backyards. He focused hard on the questions and started trailing Craig and Dinesh, whom he'd found hunting Stashes in the park. Oliver was a lone wolf on the prowl, and the diversion worked. He pushed Elena Chestnut and proud_hoser from his mind for a full thirty minutes, until a snowball smacked him hard on the right eye just outside Santabucks.

"What the—?" He shook the snow from his face and arms and wiped his eyes. The wet sludge dripped down his cheek and numbed his skin. When he'd regained his vision, he caught sight of four people darting past him, their booted footsteps pounding the sidewalk. The one bringing up the rear had long, dark, wavy hair.

Without thought or hesitation, Oliver loped after the group, sprinting like he'd never sprinted before just to keep them in his sights. When he finally caught up, he found Danny, Kevin, and Star facing off against Elena, who was brandishing a snowball, so tightly packed it was almost pure ice. Panting, Oliver ducked into the florist's doorway.

"Leave him alone," Elena shouted. "He's from Florida."

"What do you care?" asked Kevin.

"I don't. I just don't enjoy seeing you pick on people for no reason."

"Do you love him?" asked Danny in a sing-song voice. Oliver's cheeks flamed.

"Shut up," said Elena. "You're so immature."

"Elena loves Oliver. Elena loves Oliver." Danny started the chant, but, to their credit, neither Star nor Kevin joined in the chorus.

"You're five years old, Danny," Elena said. "This is not a good look for you."

"She's right," Star agreed.

Oliver reached into the snow-covered flowerpot next to the florist's door and formed a tightly-packed snowball of his own. He might have been from Florida, but North Pole was in his blood. He wound up, stepped onto the sidewalk, and hurled the snowball—smack—into Danny's face.

Kevin and Star glared at Oliver. Elena whirled around and her fiery gaze met his. He flashed a smile at her, and she returned it with her eyes.

"Bested by a Florida boy." Elena tossed her own snowball to the ground.

"Whatever, Elena." Danny wiped his face with the sleeve of his parka. "Guess who just passed you on the leader board."

She put her hands on her hips. "I was out of commission for an hour. I'll catch up."

"Good luck with that," said Kevin. "Danny wins at everything. You know that. Everyone knows that."

"Not this time," said Elena.

Star yawned, apparently bored by both the snowball shenanigans and the trash talk.

One eyebrow lifted, Danny folded his arms across his chest. "You know what they say, Elena. You sneeze you—" He stopped himself.

"What is it, Danny?" asked Oliver, stepping toward the group. "What do they say?"

"You sneeze, you...leeze?" said Elena, giggling.

"Eh," said Danny. "You know what I meant. I can't believe I wasted so much time talking to you. I've got Stashes to grab." He nodded toward the east end of Main Street, and Kevin and Star marched behind him.

Now that he and Elena had lost the buffer of Danny's unappealing competitive spirit, Oliver stood motionless, watching the others retreat with his hands behind his back. But when Danny, Star, and Kevin had rounded the corner past the video store, Elena turned toward Oliver, her eyes sparkling. "You! Nice snowball! Are you sure you're not from here?"

He held up his mittened hand. "Scout's honor." A neon sign kept flashing in his brain: this girl is proud_hoser. He had no idea what he was supposed to do with that information. Should he shun her or...not?

Uncertainty painted Elena's face as well. She peered past him, toward the other end of Main Street and their respective sporting goods stores. "Well," she said, shrugging. "I should probably catch some Stashes."

"Yeah," agreed Oliver. "I told Harper I would—"

"Yeah."

He was supposed to say good-bye in this moment. He was supposed to wave or flip her the bird or something, and they'd go their separate ways. But he didn't want to part ways. Elena had chased down Danny and his friends for Oliver. He didn't want her to leave, which was terrifying and exciting all at once.

He couldn't believe the words as they dribbled out of his mouth. "We could...team up...?" he said, shaking his head. The concept was so foreign, yet felt so impossibly right.

Elena blinked.

"I mean, if you want."

"I do want." Elena exhaled. "I'd like that...teaming up... with you."

Things had now veered to the edge of "too real" and Oliver had to return the conversation to his and Elena's particular stasis, what was normal and distant and safe. "You know, because we'll be able to help each other answer the questions. You probably know more than I do."

"Obviously," she said. "Obviously that's what I meant. The game."

"The game," he agreed.

The two of them strolled side-by-side in silence, each of them keeping their eyes on their respective phones. They ducked into several different stores on Main Street and caught their Stashes, all business. At Frank's hardware store, Oliver and Elena fielded the inevitable, "You two?" question from the storeowner himself. Frank peered at them over his half-moon reading glasses, a frown of confusion on his face. Oliver got the sense that Frank might be doubting his own eyes.

Elena handled it. "Feud's over."

"I gotta say, it's about time," said Frank, folding his arms across the bib of his overalls.

As the two of them made a loop through the residential roads north of Main Street, Elena paused in front of her house. Her parents were inside watching television, perched on opposite ends of the couch.

"You okay?" he asked.

She turned to him, knitting her brow. The beams of light from the streetlamps danced across her dark waves. "Ever since you mentioned it, I've been thinking about the plan my mom had for combining Chestnut's and Prince's." She paused. "You really think it could've worked?"

He sighed, watching her mom and dad sitting so far apart on the same piece of furniture. "I mean, from what I could see before my dad tossed the plan in the fireplace, it looked interesting." He shrugged. "Or maybe that was just wishful thinking. I don't want to go back to Florida."

She frowned. "My parents want to move to Wisconsin."

"I heard." Their eyes locked, and Oliver wondered what she meant by telling him that. Was it a test to figure out if he knew she was proud_hoser? Or was it just her opening up to him as he had opened up to her? "I wish neither of us had to leave."

A sad smile played on her lips. She drew in a deep breath and opened her mouth like she was about to say something, something important. But then she stopped herself, clamping her lips shut.

Oliver let her off the hook. Now wasn't the time to be serious. Now wasn't the time to confess truths and deal with who knew what when. This was the time to live the impossible — Oliver Prince and Elena Chestnut were enjoying each other's company. "Let's run," he said, making a move toward the end of the street. "To the park. Running always makes me feel better."

"Me, too," she said, winking. "Race you."

He took off sprinting, even though he knew how badly he was about to lose.

Chapter Twelve

Elena booked it down Spruce Street toward Main. Though Oliver had gotten a quick jump on her, she managed to pass him easily, leaving him huffing a half block behind her. She turned down Mistletoe Road, her boots beating a heavy tattoo on the pavement.

What was this night? And what did it mean that Oliver had already heard that she was moving to Wisconsin? Had he put it together that she was proud_hoser? He must have. And he was still here. He was still hanging out with her. And she was still hanging out with him, too.

Her stomach bubbling with giddy nerves, she slowed as she entered the park. A bunch of middle schoolers were on the field near the St. Nicholas statue, making snow angels. Grinning, Elena ran to them, flopped onto the snow in their vicinity, and waved her arms and legs frantically. The kids jumped up right away and abandoned her for the playground, but Elena stayed there in her frozen cocoon, eyes skyward, watching the stars blinking between the clouds.

"Hey," Oliver said a few minutes later, kicking a clump of

snow onto her leg.

Elena sat, elbows behind her, propping herself up. Oliver had leaned forward, his hands clutching his knees. He was panting. She grinned. "Rough run?"

"I'm not at your level, let's just say."

"You'll get there," she said.

"We'll see." As if near death, he flopped over onto the snow and lay near her, but a few, safe feet away.

Elena flapped her arms and legs again, digging a deeper snow angel. "You make one," she said.

"I've never done this before."

"Never ever?" she asked.

"Never ever, ever."

"Well, it's not hard."

He echoed her movements and Elena internalized their synchronized whooshing sounds as she watched the gray clouds above them sail past the stars. Then his foot hit hers, and the two of them froze like that—boot-to-boot. Suddenly the world was silent, except for the laughter of the middle schoolers in the playground.

"How much longer do I have to pretend I like being outside in this weather?" he asked.

"It's a beautiful night." Elena flipped to her side and propped herself up on her elbow. She peered over at Oliver, who was still flat on his back. His floppy copper hair had formed a halo around his head and his brown eyes gazed up at her. Neither of them had looked at their phones in a while. This was no longer a Stash Grabbing expedition. This was a date. Elena's heart thumped in her chest.

"I'm freezing," he said.

She bit her lip, wondering if she could offer to warm him up. Instead, she said, "You're such a noob."

He raised his eyebrows. "I'm a noob? Well, come to Florida sometime and we'll see how you…What's something that Floridians do that you can't do in Minnesota?"

"Surf?" she asked.

He shook his head. "I can't do that."

"Swim?"

"People swim in Minnesota."

"Wrestle alligators?"

He nodded. "That's it. That's something everyone in Florida knows how to do."

"Do you know how to skate?" Elena asked.

"Nope," he said.

"Your parents own a sporting goods store. How many of the products would you say you actually know how to use?" Elena took off a glove and ran her fingers through her own hair just to stop herself from reaching down and touching Oliver's.

He stared at her hand combing her hair as he wrinkled his brow in thought. "Hmm...three?" His eyes met hers and he winked.

Elena smiled back, but her chest tightened. "Are you really moving to Florida? Really, really?"

Oliver scrunched up his nose. "Looks like it."

"And just when I was starting to not despise you." She kept her tone light, but she knew her eyes didn't match her voice.

"The sudden lack of hatred is mutual." He bit his lip.

Not being able to take the tension anymore, Elena stood up, grabbed Oliver's gloved hands in hers, and yanked him up from the ground.

"What are we doing?" he asked.

"Skating," she said. "I'm not letting you move back to Florida until you know how to skate."

She dragged him toward the other end of the park, past the St. Nicholas statue. Just beyond that was a frozen pond, where most of the kids in town played hockey or pretended to be Olympic figure skaters.

Elena tugged Oliver onto the pond. "Come on. We're going to skate. In our boots."

Oliver, gripping her forearm, stepped gingerly onto the ice. When she knew he'd gotten his bearings, Elena led him to the middle of the pond. She plucked his hands from her arm, and then, hand in hand, pulled him around the ice. He kept up, moving his feet in synch with hers as the two of them floated over the ice like they were in a movie. She was about to comment on his prowess when Oliver's shoe hit a bump and he took them both flying.

Oliver landed facedown, and Elena lay next to him, prone, her right arm draped across his back. She turned to face him, her cheek against the ice, and he did the same. They were nose-to-nose. His swirling cloud of breath danced in front of her eyes.

She squeezed his shoulder, though she wasn't sure if he could feel the action through her mitten and his parka. "You're a good guy, Oliver Prince," she said.

"I am?" he asked, his eyes crinkling.

Elena wondered if he got the reference, if he remembered the day weeks ago when he'd told her the same, that someone had vouched for his goodness. Elena had been willing to believe that about Stashiuk4Prez, but only recently had she come to see the same thing in Oliver Prince.

Their lips were so close, they should've been kissing by now. Elena wanted that to happen, she wanted him to make it happen. Kevin Snow would've easily been on the case by now. But part of her wasn't ready for that yet. This wasn't their moment to kiss. Not tonight. Not with so much left unsaid. Maybe Oliver felt that, too.

She pushed herself up on all fours, stood, and helped Oliver from the ice. As they paused there in the middle of the pond, all four mittened hands clutching one another,

Elena asked, "Do you have a date to the dance tomorrow?" She chewed on her bottom lip. Everything was now out in the open. There was no more hiding behind fake names and avatars.

Oliver's eyes sparkled. "I'm kind of meeting someone there."

"Me, too," she said seriously. "And I'm really, really looking forward to it. Really."

"Same," he said. "She's pretty special, from what I've been lead to believe."

"I don't know," said Elena. "I bet she's the evilest witch in all the land."

Oliver frowned. "Reports of her evilness have been greatly exaggerated."

She squeezed as hard as she could through their mittens. "Well, I know you have a date and everything, but maybe save me a dance."

He shrugged. "We'll see. No promises."

She touched his calf with her foot. "All I have to do right now is sweep your leg and you'll be stuck here on this ice until spring."

"What I said about my date not being an evil witch? I take that back."

She tugged on his hands, dragging herself in close to his chest. They were cheek-to-cheek now, his hot breath tickling her ear. She let her lips graze his lobe ever so slightly as she reached into his coat pocket and pulled out Harper's phone. She held it up, backing away. "I'll return this for you. I want to make sure Harper's okay."

After they said an awkward good-bye on the shore— Elena told Oliver to make sure to stretch his calves when he got home—she ran to her house, got her parents' car, and drove to Harper's.

She found her friend on the sectional couch in her family

room, surrounded by various snack foods, right leg propped up on the ottoman, watching *Can't Buy Me Love*. A pile of DVDs sat next to the TV. "Courtesy of Sam," said Harper. "I reminded him that we have Netflix and Amazon and On Demand and a million other ways to watch things. He went off on a tirade about how those services always try to direct you to their own product. That's when I kicked him out." She nodded toward the movie, where Patrick Dempsey was mowing the lawn. "This movie is great, though. Don't tell Sam that."

Elena lowered herself gingerly to the couch, making sure not to disrupt Harper's leg. "How's your ankle?"

"Broken," said Harper. "Looks okay, though. I probably won't need surgery or anything."

"How are you feeling? Does it hurt?"

"Not anymore." Harper shook the bottle of painkillers on the end table next to her.

"And can I get you anything?"

"Absolutely nothing. Sam has been an amazing nurse." Harper nodded toward the TV. "You can watch with me, though. Cheesy rom-coms are no fun to sit through alone."

"True story." Elena tried to focus on the screen. It wasn't working. Young Patrick Dempsey wasn't a good enough distraction. His floppy hair couldn't hold a candle to Oliver's.

"How was your night?" asked Harper, watching Patrick Dempsey scoot around on a riding mower.

Elena chuckled. "Interesting. Much better than yours, I'm fairly certain."

Harper shook her head. "My night has been pretty good, actually. The doctor gave me the strong stuff. But I can tell even through my narcotics haze that something's bothering you."

"Not bothering me," said Elena. "But I do have something on my mind." She exhaled. "After you left, I spent all evening hanging out with Oliver. And I liked it. A lot."

Harper flicked off the TV completely. Good-bye, Patrick Dempsey. She pivoted her torso as much as she physically could without moving her leg to face Elena. "What?" When Elena didn't respond right away, Harper repeated, "What?"

"We hung out...catching Stashes and stuff." Elena shrugged. "It was a lot of fun. We had sort of a moment, and...I should probably start at the beginning."

"Please do," Harper said.

"You know how I've been playing Stash Grab?"

"Like everyone."

"Well, I started chatting with some guy right in the beginning. We really hit it off, like to the point where we made plans to meet up at the Valentine's dance—I'd wear a yellow dress and he'd bring me a yellow rose."

"You're living in a rom-com."

"It gets more rom-commy." Elena grinned in spite of herself. "I figured out at my Stash Grab Dash event that the guy I'd been chatting with the whole time was Oliver Prince."

Harper spilled half her popcorn. "Uh, go on," she said, attempting to wrangle the loose kernels.

"And tonight I realized that Oliver, somewhere along the line, had figured out he'd been chatting with me. And yet...he was still there hanging out with me for hours."

"And you with him."

"Yeah." Elena sighed.

"You said you two had a 'moment.' What kind of moment?"

Elena closed her eyes, picturing the scene. "We were goofing around on the ice in the park, and we fell next to each other, like nose-to-nose—"

Harper clapped her hands in excitement. "My stomach is literally full of butterflies right now. You and Oliver, oh my God. You guys kissed."

"Who kissed?" shouted Sam from the basement.

"Mind your own business, loser!" yelled Harper. She turned to Elena again. "How was it?" she asked in a softer voice.

"We didn't kiss," said Elena. "And we never came right out and said we knew the other was the person we'd been chatting with, but it was definitely implied, and I think we were on the same page—tomorrow night, the Valentine's dance. I'm wearing a yellow dress, and he's bringing me a yellow rose."

"A yellow dress! Just like *How to Lose a Guy in 10 Days*!"

"That's why I bought it, obviously," Elena said. "Anyway, tomorrow night, all will be revealed."

"With sexy results!" Harper screeched.

Elena tossed a pillow at her.

"I have a broken ankle. You have to be nice to me." Harper's face got serious. "I'm proud of you," she said. "And happy. You never go after what you want." She shoved a handful of popcorn into her mouth.

"Yes, I do," Elena said.

"I mean it," Harper said, her mouth full. "You usually don't fight for yourself, but here you are, going after Oliver Prince."

"I fight for what I want." She was a strong, independent woman who always stuck up for herself. Of course she was.

Harper took a moment to swallow. "Elena, no, you don't. Your parents want you to quit the track team to work at the store more, you do it. No question. They want you to give up the school trip. Done. They tell you you're going to have to move before your senior year. No problem. I like that for once you've found something—someone—you want, and you're going after him. You're going to wear that yellow dress and kiss Oliver Prince's face, and it's going to be amazing."

"You make me sound like a doormat."

"You're not a doormat, and I know the stuff with your parents is complicated, but you always let life happen to you. It's like the whole Kevin Snow thing last year; you let him hold the reins the entire time. 'Sure, Kevin, you want to make out tonight? Let's do that. Oh, you're done with me? Fine. No big deal. We can still be friends.'"

"I did want to make out with him." She blushed, remembering their few nights of passion, or whatever that was—in the back of the video store and at one of Harper's parties. He was a tool, but he was a hot tool.

"I don't doubt that, but you did it on his terms. You live your entire life on everybody else's terms."

Elena glowered. "You do think I'm a pushover."

"I think you're very concerned about not making waves." Harper grabbed another handful of popcorn. "But I like that you're going after Oliver. That relationship won't make anybody's life easy. It's messy—your parents won't like it, neither will his parents. You're both leaving the state soon. You're not going after him because it's rational and right. You're going after him because you want to."

Elena rolled her eyes. She couldn't believe her friend saw her this way. "Okay, you want to know something else I want? I want you to go with me tomorrow night," said Elena. "That's part of the reason I came here tonight. Will you be my moral support at the Valentine's dance? Because I'm nervous as hell."

"Of course!" Harper said. "I wouldn't miss this for the world."

• • •

Oliver's feet had not touched the ground in going on twenty hours.

He had never done drugs before, and he didn't drink

much, but this had to be what it felt like to be under the influence of…something. One time his mom had had a root canal, and she'd still been woozy from the laughing gas when Oliver had driven her home. She'd kept beaming at the drivers of passing cars and pointing out the loveliness in everything she saw—police cars, dumpsters, their neighbor's saucy new muumuu. That's how Oliver felt in the wake of his evening with Elena. He was suddenly able to appreciate the beauty in a loud, floral housedress.

He was a marionette, the strings lifting his various body parts to the sky, fixing his posture, lightening his load. His eyes gleamed and grinned with every bouncy step.

In social studies first period, he blushed when Elena strolled through the door, but relaxed when he saw that her cheeks were similarly pink. She fluttered her fingers at him with a shy smile, and he returned the gesture. Last night wasn't a dream. It had really happened. He and Elena had truly connected.

All day long, the universe stayed on his side. During lunch, his counselor called him in to talk about college plans—a school in Colorado had heard about the Stash Grab app and was interested in speaking to him. He aced his Latin quiz during seventh period (Thank you, Elena). In calculus, he solved a problem correctly before anybody else.

On his way home after school, he realized he was skipping, and he couldn't stop. Skipping was his new normal gait. He sashayed through his front door, thinking he was alone, but he was met by a sadly familiar scene—his dad snoring on the couch in the living room, surrounded by empty beer cans and another stack of paper. Even that couldn't kill his buzz. Practically floating, Oliver cleaned up the remnants of his dad's afternoon—recycling the cans and trashing the potato chip bags. The papers today, however, did give him pause. They weren't plans from Mrs. Chestnut this time. They were the divorce papers from his mom.

Oliver read through the contract dissolving his parents' marriage. They would split custody of Oliver and Regina, who could choose to live full-time with either parent. They were, after all, already seventeen.

He glanced at his dad, who had a trail of dried drool running from his mouth to his chin. Maybe he'd want to stay here. Maybe now that his marriage to Oliver's mom was for sure over, he'd be willing to give North Pole another shot. Oliver needed that to be true.

Trip's phone buzzed and he shot up to a seated position, grasping for the phone on the couch next to him. Oliver dug it out from between the cushions and handed the phone to his dad.

"Jenny?" His dad ran a hand over his bald head. "Jenny, talk to me."

Oliver averted his eyes and tiptoed into the front hallway. He wasn't supposed to hear this conversation between his parents. He hid behind the doorjamb, however, and spied on his father's end of the chat.

"Jenny, please," his dad said. "I'm going to close the store and move back to Florida. We can work this out…No, we haven't grown apart…We can still—" He tossed the phone to the table.

Oliver stepped back into the room. "Dad, are you o—"

His dad snatched up his phone and his coat and dashed out the front door, without a word.

Still, Oliver's mood didn't dip, at least not that much. His dad would eventually realize the divorce was really happening. He'd wake up and start planning for his future without Oliver's mom. Maybe he'd finally talk to Elena's mom about her plan for the stores.

Maybe it would mean Elena could stay in North Pole, too.

Oliver showered and shoved on his best pair of gray

pants, which he ironed himself, and a pink dress shirt with a pink and green plaid tie. It was a Valentine's dance after all. He combed his hair and borrowed some of his dad's cologne, which smelled like ginger and cedar. Then, right before seven o'clock, he ventured out into the night.

Snow had just started falling, and, even though he could hardly remember what the world looked like without snow at this point, Oliver welcomed it tonight. Snowflakes danced in the streetlights and covered the gray slush that had been collecting since the last storm. North Pole felt tonight like it did back in December before all the Christmas decorations had been tarnished or deflated and when everyone's spirits were high. All around him, people sauntered in the same direction—in pairs, groups, or alone—probably on their way to the Valentine's dance at school.

Oliver, however, took a detour toward Main Street and stopped in at the flower shop. He had a rose to buy. Bobbi Moore stood behind the counter, helping Kevin Snow pick out a corsage for his date. "A special bouquet for a special lady," she said, as she tied a bow around the clear plastic box.

Kevin grumbled. "Not that special." He tossed a few bucks onto the counter and nodded to Oliver as he trudged toward the door.

Oliver stepped to the counter and laid his hands on top. "Hi, Bobbi," he said, hoping he still possessed whatever magic he'd been sporting all day. Bobbi was not pleased to see him.

She sneered. "People are still coming in my backyard at all hours of the night."

"I'm sorry," said Oliver. "I told my sister—"

"You said the situation would be fixed." She folded her arms.

"I know," he said. "I thought it was, but…good news is, the game is over on Sunday—"

"So, two more days of this crap, and my fence is still

broken, by the way. My dogs keep getting out. They're running all over town." Oliver did not remind her that, fence or no, her dogs always ran wild through the streets of North Pole. Bobbi glared in his general direction. "What can I do for you tonight?"

Oliver cleared his throat. She was a businesswoman. This was a business transaction. Of course she'd fill his order. "I need a yellow rose."

She shook her head. "No yellow roses."

"Not one?" Oliver peered past her toward the flower-filled refrigerator behind the counter. There was a bucket full of yellow roses right there, plopped in the middle of the fridge. "What about those?"

"Nope," she said. "Sorry. Not for you."

"I'll pay you extra—" Oliver reached into his pocket and pulled out a wad of cash. He'd give her all he had—twenty, forty dollars for one rose.

"I don't want your money," she said. "Get people to stop jumping my fence *like you promised* and I'll give you all the roses you want for free."

Where was he going to get a yellow rose now? The only option left was the grocery store, which was all the way on the other side of town. He was going to be so late for the dance. He dashed down Main Street and into Ludlum's. There he found, not a yellow rose, but some dyed yellow carnations. They'd have to do. He even bought a full bouquet just to account for the fact that he was showing up with carnations. If a rose was the Cadillac of flowers, a carnation was the Ford Fiesta.

When he exited Ludlum's the snow no longer lifted his spirits. This night was supposed to be perfect. He was supposed to show up on time and with a yellow rose. Here he was running a half hour late and armed with stupid carnations.

Letting the bouquet hang down to his side, he squinted

into the snow and marched down Main Street, where he'd cut down Spruce Street to head toward the school. He passed his dad's store, which was empty except for Craig, who was working. He crossed Main Street and passed Chestnut's, where Elena's dad was manning the counter in the deserted shop. Just past their store, he heard yelling, which was coming from the alley behind The Chinese Restaurant.

Oliver's first instinct was not usually to play real-life superhero, but Elena had told him he was a good guy, so he decided to live up to that description. He crossed Spruce and turned down the alley as a woman shouted, "You can't just come in and out of this whenever you feel like it. You're jerking me around."

And then a man's voice said, "I'm trying to figure things out."

"We all are."

The man's voice belonged to his father. Oliver would know his gravelly tone anywhere. He padded down the alley, his boots scraping against the gravel. When he reached the back of The Chinese Restaurant, he found two figures—his dad and Elena's mom—leaning against the back wall of the restaurant, kissing.

Oliver tried to stop the squeak from his throat, but he couldn't. His dad pulled away from Mrs. Chestnut and whipped toward him. Their eyes met. His dad's were puffy and bloodshot. Mrs. Chestnut clamped her hand to her mouth.

Oliver dropped his carnations and ran.

Chapter Thirteen

The yellow dress was starting to itch.

That, and Elena was freezing in it. What had she been thinking, wearing a chiffon gown to a dance in the middle of February in Minnesota?

She parked next to the refreshments table and busied herself with a cup of punch, wishing it were hot cocoa, while she stared at the entrance to the school gym, not even pretending like she wasn't full-on watching every single person who came and went through that door.

There was a clock over the door, a visual reminder of time passing. Oliver was five minutes late, then ten, then fifteen, now he was over forty-five minutes late. She checked her phone. No messages.

Harper, whom Elena had sent away when she'd offered to hover near the punch bowl with her, came back to check in every ten minutes or so. Wearing her boot cast and wielding one crutch, she'd been attempting to dance with the likes of Danny and Star and the rest of their usual crowd. Harper flopped onto the chair next to the refreshments table. "It's tiring dancing with a broken ankle. Stick a fork in me."

Elena dragged a second chair over to Harper, and helped her friend elevate her bad foot.

"Still no word from Oliver?" Harper asked, massaging her calf muscle.

Elena shook her head and focused again on the door.

"He'll be here," said Harper. "He's just running late."

"Mmm-hmm." A niggling voice deep down kept reminding her that this was on-brand behavior for his family. Never trust a Prince. It's a lesson she'd been taught her whole life.

"You guys had a great time together last night," Harper reminded her.

Elena was on the verge of sobbing. They had. They'd had a wonderful time. He'd even told her in so many words that he was excited about the dance tonight. He'd waved to her at school. Everything had been clipping along nicely.

So, why was he not here?

Was last night a big ruse? Had it merely been him lulling her into a false sense of security before standing her up?

"He's not blowing you off," said Harper, reading Elena's mind.

Elena pressed her lips together.

"He wouldn't do that." Harper reached into her bag and pulled out her phone. "I'll text him."

Elena grabbed for Harper's phone. "Don't."

"I'm doing it," she said, fingers moving across her screen. "It's done." She dropped the phone onto her lap.

The two girls stared at the door, waiting and watching.

"Still no text?" asked Elena when three minutes had passed.

"Nope."

The second hand had journeyed around the clock face twice more, when the gym door creaked open. Elena straightened up, her breath catching in her chest.

She saw the copper hair first and her heart sped up, but her body deflated when she realized it wasn't attached to Oliver's head. The hair belonged to Regina, who waltzed into the dance on the arm of Stan Stashiuk.

"Regina and Stash?" whispered Harper.

Elena glanced down at her friend, whose eyes were wide and wounded.

"That's who she's been seeing?" asked Harper.

Elena crouched down and hugged Harper, who brushed her off.

"I'm fine," Harper said, squaring her shoulders. She waved Regina over. Elena thought she looked like Don Corleone holding court before his daughter's wedding. She made a mental note to tell Sam about her quick-drawn *Godfather* reference. He'd be so proud.

Regina whispered something to Stash, and then sauntered over to Elena and Harper. "Hi, ladies."

"You and Stash?" said Harper.

Regina backed up a step. "Uh…yeah." She frowned. "I'm sorry, Harper. It's…you knew I was seeing someone else."

Harper shook her head, like she was shaking away her hurt. Elena braced herself for a big blow-up, but instead Harper stuck her chin out and said, "Well, I'm not surprised. I've seen the way you guys look at each other."

Regina grinned.

"I can't blame you, honestly. He's a freaking professional hockey player who cares about bettering the lives of needy children. You could do worse."

"I could do way worse," Regina said.

"You could've shown up on the arm of, like, one of the Sugarplum Sweethearts or something, in which case, I would've had to murder you." Harper shuddered, and Elena patted her hand. The Sugarplum Sweetheart beauty contest was never not going to be a sore spot for her friend.

Grinning, Regina glanced back at Stan Stashiuk. "Stash and I just…we bonded."

Harper shrugged. "I get it. And it's not like you weren't honest with me about your feelings. It's tough to see someone you like with another person, is all. It's jarring."

"I'm sorry," said Regina. "I should've told you before the dance. We had been taking it slow, but now…"

Harper waved her off. "You can make it up to me by telling us where the hell your brother is tonight."

Elena's stomach dropped. Here was the moment of truth.

Regina frowned. "Ollie?"

"You have another brother?" asked Harper.

Regina shrugged. "Where else would he be? He's at home."

"You're sure?" asked Elena.

"I just left him." She scrunched up her nose. "Was he supposed to meet you here?"

Harper cut in. "Yeah. He told me we'd hang out."

Regina rolled her eyes. "Sorry. My antisocial brother is at home in a T-shirt and a pair of pajama pants. He looked like he was in for the night."

Elena swallowed, clutching her phone. The idea that something terrible had happened to Oliver had crossed her mind earlier in the night. Perhaps he had been hit by a car or a snowmobile or one of the Christmas trollies that ran up and down Main Street. How tragic would that have been, for the love of Elena's young life to have been snuffed out before they could profess their undying devotion to each other?

Though all of that would've been preferable to being stood up by a pajama pants-wearing liar.

"What's he doing at home?" asked Elena, beginning to seethe.

"Playing video games." Regina shrugged. "My dad caved

and gave him his computer back."

Elena nodded. Oliver had chosen his computer over her. In truth, however, he had never chosen her at all. He was never going to come to the dance in the first place. He was Regina's anti-social brother who loved video games more than human companionship.

"Thanks, Regina," Elena said.

Regina nodded and dashed off to find Stan Stashiuk, and Elena stood rooted to the floor, still staring at the door.

"You gonna go after him?" Harper said.

Elena glowered at her friend. "Are you kidding me?"

"Don't you want to confront him? Give him a piece of your mind?" Harper gestured toward Regina. "Like I just did with Regina. I could've ignored her all night and sat here fuming while I endured watching her and Stash dance together, but I didn't. I called her over, told her what was bothering me, and we worked it out. Maybe you and Oliver can work it out."

"There's nothing to work out," said Elena. "He was supposed to show up, and he didn't. He's at home playing video games and not thinking about me, so I'm going to stay here and dance and not think about him."

She drained her punch and marched onto the dance floor, where she joined the group Harper had been bopping around with previously—Danny, Star, Kevin, and Marley.

Danny nudged her in the side. "Who are you here with?"

"No one," she said. She was going to leave it at that, but instead chose the nuclear option. If Oliver was going to stand her up, then she was going to take him down with her. She was not going to let him hide, consequence-free, behind his computer. "I was supposed to meet Oliver Prince here, but he blew me off. Never trust a Prince," she added.

She glanced up at Kevin Snow, who was watching her with his usual sultry stare. Elena knew he looked at everyone like that, so she didn't kid herself that it meant anything, but she pretended it did. Tonight she needed to feel like someone found her attractive, even if it was just Kevin.

When he asked her to dance later, she said yes. She wrapped her arms around his neck and breathed in his sweaty scent under a thick layer of sandalwood body spray. It brought her back to a few months ago, when the odd dalliance with Kevin was enough for Elena—pre-Stash Grab, pre-Oliver.

But she'd never truly had Oliver, and Stashiuk4Prez was just a mirage.

She decided to lean into whatever this frivolity with Kevin Snow was, because that was what she wanted, at least for tonight. And she was going to get something she wanted for once, thank you, Harper.

"Where's your date?" Elena whispered in his ear.

He shrugged.

Elena decided that if Kevin wasn't worried about it, she wouldn't worry about it, either.

After the dance, she and Harper trudged through the snow to Danny's house for an after party. Elena ran into Kevin there, in Danny's mom's room, which was serving as the coatroom. He waved, about to leave and find something to drink or someone else to make out with or who knew, whatever.

To prove to herself, and Harper in absentia, that Elena sometimes did go after what she wanted, and to prove to herself that Oliver Prince meant less than nothing to her, she stepped right up to Kevin Snow, placed her hand on his chest, and touched her lips to his.

His mouth responded with its familiar vigor, and Elena tried to keep up, but her mind kept flashing to Oliver and how this was what she'd imagined doing with him tonight. She was doing it with stupid Kevin Snow instead, which was pretty much the opposite of what she wanted. She'd been on this ride before, and she'd promised herself she'd never do it again. A few months ago, the last time she and Kevin had hooked up during the Saturday night classic movie show, Elena had run home crying from the video store. She swore then that the next person she'd kiss would be someone who liked her back. That wasn't this. Elena put her hands on Kevin's chest and pushed him away.

"Thanks, Kevin," she said, a lump in her throat.

"Any time," he responded.

"You should go find your date, probably."

He shrugged. "Find me later, if you want."

She didn't want. She'd never want. Elena grabbed her coat and booked it out Danny's front door. Kissing Kevin had helped nothing. It was like trying to smother a burning building with a dishtowel.

• • •

"You're an idiot and an asshole."

The text from Harper arrived around ten-thirty. Oliver glanced at it and then flipped his phone face down on his desk.

He knew what he was. He didn't need Harper to tell him.

Having no idea where to go or what to do, he'd taken off running after finding his dad kissing Elena's mom. He'd considered busting into the dance and telling Elena about it. He'd considered fleeing the town completely, hopping the next plane for Florida. What actually happened, however, was that his dad caught up with him, grabbed his arm, and forced Oliver to listen to his side of the story.

"You didn't see what you thought you saw."

Oliver's mind kept circling back to the thing he definitely both saw and thought he saw. "You weren't kissing Elena's mom? You were giving her mouth-to-mouth? You were showing her your fillings, up close and personal?"

Shaking, Trip closed his eyes. "It was nothing," he said. "We'd had a few drinks, things got heated. It was a mistake. A one-time mistake. Emily and I both acknowledge that."

"What were you doing getting drinks with her anyway?" asked Oliver.

His dad blew out a deep breath. "It's complicated. Our history is complicated. We were talking as friends. That's it."

Oliver shook his head and took off running again. He couldn't stand here listening to this. His dad had kissed Elena's mom. Why it had happened didn't matter. Elena wouldn't care about the why. Her dad wasn't going to care about the why. Oliver sure didn't.

He and his dad met up again on the front steps of their house. Oliver stood panting on the top stair, while his dad gazed up at him from the walkway. "How can I make this up to you?" asked Trip.

Nothing was going to make this up to him. Oliver was screwed here. He couldn't be with Elena after this. There was no way. They were doomed. He had caught their parents kissing, and he couldn't tell Elena about it. How could he break that news to her? His parents' marriage was already ruined. He wasn't going to help destroy another one.

Oliver's only recourse was to fade away, bow out, not show up to the dance. Elena would hate him, everyone would hate him, but so what? How was that different than his life up to this point? He was going back to Florida soon anyway. His life in North Pole was over no matter what he did.

"I want my computer back," said Oliver.

"Deal," said Trip, immediately.

"Now." Oliver glared at his father.

Within five minutes, Oliver was up in his room, his dress pants and shirt abandoned in a ball on his closet floor. He set his laptop on his desk, opened it, and pressed the power button. The room whirred with sound—the motor of the machine, the pinging of the alerts he'd missed over the past several weeks, the subtle clicks as his hard drive revved up. Oliver no longer had to be alone with his thoughts. He was back in his happy, safe, virtual space.

His first instinct was to check out Stash Grab, but that game had been ruined for him. It was now a stark reminder of what could've been. Instead, he opened up a new campaign in Wizard War and lost himself in a pretend world of magic and mayhem.

He received one text from Harper around seven-fifty. "Where are you?"

He ignored it and blasted an enemy wizard in the chest with a kill spell.

A text from Regina came in a few minutes later. "Harper and Elena Chestnut are looking for you?"

He stole a quick glance at the message and accepted a side quest from a crone in the woods.

A few hours later, after the dance was long over, he got the "You're an idiot and an asshole" text from Harper.

He didn't care. He couldn't care.

He was doing everyone a kindness, including himself.

Elena would hate him for a few days, and then she'd move on. Hating him was nothing new to her, anyway. She'd be fine.

He, Oliver, would be fine, too. He had his computer back. He could lose himself in his games and projects again. He'd flirted with real life emotion, and he'd been burned. He wouldn't make that mistake again.

Much later that night, a witch invited him to her private hut. This kind of thing happened all the time in Wizard War. The huts were meant to be used for private campaign planning conversations, but most people used them to hook up. They were virtual sex shacks. Oliver had previously turned down any hut propositions. He cared only about the campaigns, improving his score, and winning the game. But tonight he wanted to forget, so he clicked yes.

His avatar was transported to a fully decorated one-room hut. There was a green couch and a table with two chairs. Pictures of cats filled most of the wall space. A few seconds later, a witch popped into the room. She was blond, short, and muscular. She reminded him of proud_hoser's avatar. (And Harper, too, now that he stopped to think about it, which was an uncomfortable realization.)

"Hi?" he said, hopeful. What if this witch was Elena? What if she somehow knew he had been playing this game, found him, and invited him to hang out in a safe, virtual sex shack?

"I'm Gilda the Glad," boomed the witch's voice through his speakers. The woman sounded like she'd been smoking a pack a day for the past fifty years.

"Sorry," Oliver stammered, fiddling with the game controls. "I thought you were someone else."

With a snap, he rejoined his campaign and vowed to stay away from any and all private huts. He wasn't emotionally ready for romance, real or imagined.

Unless it involved Elena.

Chapter Fourteen

"Have a nice day, Craig," Elena said.

Eyes wary, Craig picked up his shopping bag, one of the last ones left with the Chestnut's logo on it. He, like everyone else in North Pole, was getting in on the going-out-of-business sale. Craig paused, waiting.

"Is there anything else I can help you with?" Elena asked.

Craig shook his head, wide-eyed terror on his face. "You said have a nice day."

"And…?" Elena said.

"Is the apocalypse upon us?" Craig asked. "You were polite to me. You're never polite to me."

"I'll revert to my old ways if you don't vamoose," she said, shooing him toward the door.

Craig grinned, wiping his brow. "Now, that's the Elena I know and tolerate."

Once the door had shut behind him, Elena ripped an extra bit of paper off the receipt printer and tossed it into the recycling bin. After the dance last night, she no longer had the energy or the desire to bicker with Craig. Stashiuk4Prez was a lie. Oliver Prince was the jerk who had stood her up. She had kissed Kevin Snow—again. Elena had lost all meaning in her life.

The store was closing. Her family was moving to Wisconsin. She might as well get used to it. What was left for her here, anyway?

She glanced across the street to Prince's, where Regina was outside hanging a sign announcing the big end-of-Stash-Grab party tomorrow morning. Today was the final day of the game. Tomorrow it'd all be over—someone else, someone besides Elena, probably Danny—would win the plane tickets, and it wouldn't matter, because Elena was moving to Wisconsin. What was one final spring break with her friends to her? Yeah, she'd wanted to go. Yeah, she'd dreamed about how much fun it would be. But it wasn't going to happen, so why pretend?

She watched her fellow townsfolk scurry along the sidewalk, which had turned slippery after an overnight post-snow deep freeze. During the storm last night, North Pole had been lively, full of motion. Today, despite the people skidding across the ice, the town was static, still, raw. The icicles didn't drip. Water didn't rush down the gutters. Elena and her town were frozen in suspended animation, waiting for life to happen.

Around dinnertime, her mom came rushing in, disrupting Elena's mind-numbing run on one of the treadmills in the home gym section. Her mom tossed her purse to the counter and sighed. "Your father." She balled her hands into fists.

Her meditative state ruined, Elena hopped off the treadmill and hid her mom's purse under the register. "What happened?" asked Elena. She noticed her mom's eyes were red, and so were her cheeks. She had been crying.

"He just—argh!" her mom growled, banging on the counter. Eyes wild, she told Elena, "I figured out a way for us to keep the store and stay in town, but your dad's pettiness—"

Elena's dad, hand bandaged past his wrist, burst through the front door at just that moment. "My pettiness? You kissed Trip Prince."

Dinesh, who'd stopped just outside the store and had been about to come in, turned tail and ran across the street.

A warm sense of dread flooded Elena's body and knocked her out of her emotional deep freeze. "What happened?" she asked through a clenched jaw.

"Well, your mother kissed Trip," her dad explained.

"I got that," said Elena.

Her mom, who'd given up on trying to explain things to her husband, apparently, spoke directly to Elena. "We kissed for two seconds," she said. "And"—she scowled at her husband—"it's something we both acknowledge was a stupid mistake."

"Consider me a member of that club." Tom Chestnut raised his hand.

"It's also not something we should be discussing in front of our teenage daughter."

"Too late for that now," Elena said. "Tell me what happened."

Elena's parents stood in front of the counter, her mom on one side and her dad on the other, like Elena was the judge presiding over this courtroom. Her mom pled her case. "I'd had this idea for a while that we should apologize to Trip, to see if he'd be willing to let bygones be bygones after decades of separation and recombine our stores like the old days. Because the way things are now—with the new Wal-Mart outside of town, plus Amazon and the fact that you can buy anything you need online—neither our store nor Prince's would survive with the way things have been going."

"And then you kissed him," said Tom.

Elena's mom rolled her eyes at her daughter. Elena

understood the meaning behind this gesture was, "Men. Am I right?" Elena scowled. She wasn't on her mom's side. She had kissed someone who was not Elena's father.

Her mom continued. "I admit that I went behind your dad's back and contacted Trip. But your dad refused to listen to my ideas, and I have as much history with Trip as he does."

"And now you're kissing him. Again." Tom folded his arms.

Elena frowned. This was not a productive conversation. They weren't getting anywhere. "Dad, let Mom finish."

"Thank you," her mom said. "So, I'd gone to Trip a few weeks ago and suggested that we merge the stores." Elena pictured the papers Oliver had found burning to a crisp in the Princes' fireplace. "Trip was completely against the idea."

"Credit where credit's due," mumbled Elena's dad.

"But then last night, I got a call from him out of nowhere. He was really upset, and he wanted to meet. I told your dad before I even said yes"—she gestured toward her husband—"so it was all on the up-and-up."

"Sure it was," Elena's dad said.

Elena shot him a look to keep quiet.

"Well, your dad forbade me to meet with Trip." Emily Chestnut shook her head at her husband.

"I didn't forbid you. I asked you not to go because I was worried about what might happen, and apparently my concern was warranted."

"Okay, you didn't 'forbid' me, but you were kind of a jerk about it." She turned to Elena. "I told your dad this could be good for us, this could let us keep the store and stay in North Pole, but he said he didn't trust Trip. Trip had ulterior motives, as far as your dad was concerned. I said, well, don't you trust me?' Your dad said no, and then I tossed a vase to the floor and stormed out."

"I cut myself trying to clean up her mess." Her dad held

up his bandaged hand.

Elena sighed. Her parents were children. Maybe that's what love did, no matter how old you were. Elena, after all, wasn't so innocent herself. She'd gotten so upset last night that she went down the path she'd promised herself she'd never take again—Kevin Snow Road.

"I met Trip at The Chinese Restaurant," said Elena's mom. "I assumed he'd invited me there to talk business, that he finally realized we both needed to do something to juice up our stores, but really he just needed a friend. His wife sent him divorce papers yesterday."

"Oh." Elena's hand went to her mouth. Oliver had known his parents were divorcing, but seeing it in writing had to have been a real blow. She shook her head. Oliver blew her off last night. He hadn't bothered to tell her what had happened before standing her up. Even if he had been upset, he could've called. He could've texted. She would've understood.

"Trip and I had a few drinks—which, maybe that wasn't my best move, maybe I should've stayed more clearheaded, but whatever. What's done is done. The two of us started to argue about shit from the past. He was obviously mad at me for running off with Tom. I was mad at him because he'd conveniently forgotten how absent he'd been during our engagement. Mr. Wong told us to get out of his restaurant, so we did. We went into the alley and fought some more. Things got heated, and we kissed. For a fraction of a second. I went home and told your dad everything immediately. There was no hiding it, anyway. Trip's son caught us." Elena's mom shuddered.

"Oliver caught you?" Elena's heart sped up.

Unmoved by his wife's story, Elena's dad had folded his arms across his chest. "I can't believe you kissed him. Trip is probably crowing right now."

"He's not. I promise you. He's sad. He misses his wife."

Elena held up a hand to shush her parents. "Oliver saw you?"

Her mom shook her head. "I feel terrible. We heard this gasp, and Trip and I turned toward the end of the alley. There was Oliver, holding a bouquet of yellow flowers. He spun around and ran, and Trip bolted after him."

Elena's jaw dropped. "He had yellow flowers?"

"Dropped them right there in the alley. Trip trampled them trying to catch Oliver."

"Oh," she said again. Elena picked up a rag from under the cash register and started wiping down the counter.

Oliver had had a bouquet of yellow flowers.

"The plan would've never worked anyway," said Elena's dad.

"You don't know that," her mom argued. "It was worth a try at least."

But Oliver hadn't called her. He'd left Elena alone at the dance. He'd stood her up.

"Teaming up with Trip Prince." Elena's dad shook his head.

"You two were best friends," her mom reminded her husband, "until you ran off with his fiancée. Trip is not the bad guy here. At least he's not the only bad guy."

Oliver probably hadn't called because he'd just seen his dad kissing Elena's mom. Maybe he hadn't known what to say, how to start that conversation? Especially since Elena had a track record of biting Oliver's head off when he delivered bad news.

She pulled out her phone and opened up a new text conversation. She was going to write him, Oliver, for real. No more hiding behind their Stash Grab personae.

"Call me. Please. We need to talk."

She sent the message and waited, dusting the pictures behind the counter, enduring more of her parents' circular conversation about the kiss and the business and moving to Wisconsin. She paused on the sign that said, "We reserve the right to deny service to any Prince."

Elena checked her phone. Still nothing.

She sent him one more message: "I know about the kiss."

Elena ducked into the basketball aisle and started stacking shoeboxes. One minute. No new messages. Two minutes. Still nothing. Three, four, five.

What was she doing? Again, she was waiting around for someone else to give her what she wanted. She was wasting time. She'd put herself out there. She'd sent the text. He was the one who'd blown her off last night, and he was the one who was ignoring her now. Well, forget that, and forget him.

She stepped out of the aisle and stood, arms akimbo like Wonder Woman, facing her parents, who had moved on from the kiss and were now calmly discussing the logistics of Elena's mother's plan. "I've gotta go," Elena said.

Her dad checked the Picabo Street clock on the wall behind the counter. "The store's open for two more hours."

"You can handle it." She held up her phone. "I'm going to win Stash Grab and I'm going on spring break."

. . .

Oliver murdered a wizened old warlock with a flame-thrower spell, but he took no joy in it.

He'd been playing Wizard War for almost twenty-four hours now and the side effects he'd come here for—distraction, numbness, a powerful sense of control—had worn off.

He exited the game and leaned back in his desk chair, running his hands through his gnarly hair. He hadn't slept. He hadn't showered. He'd only eaten the food his sister brought him, when she remembered to bring him anything. It didn't matter. He wasn't hungry, and his taste buds were dead.

Oliver flipped over his phone and reread the messages Elena had sent him a few hours ago. She wanted to talk. She knew about the kiss.

Well, so what? The kiss was the problem, wasn't it? Her knowing about it didn't change the fact that it had happened.

"Oliver?" His dad knocked on the door and entered without waiting for a response. Trip wrinkled his nose as he stepped over the threshold. "It's a little...ripe...in here."

Oliver folded his arms across his chest.

"Have you left this room once today?"

Oliver scowled at his father.

"I want to talk about what happened." Trip perched on the edge of Oliver's bed, the bed he hadn't slept in all night because he'd been on the computer, trying to forget about the kiss his dad wanted to chat about now. "I wasn't lying when I said the kiss didn't mean anything, but that doesn't mean it wasn't stupid."

Oliver reached back, his finger hovering over the mouse pad on his computer. He longed to open up Wizard War again, just to get away from this conversation, to escape. He caught himself, though, and spun around to face his dad. "You're right. It *was* stupid."

"I was having a rough night, what with your mom filing for divorce and everything..." Trip scratched the top of his head. Oliver wondered if his dad used to run his fingers through his own hair, back when he had hair, during nervous moments like Oliver did. "I know the divorce is the right thing. Don't get me wrong. It's just...I'm not good at failure."

Oliver raised his eyebrows.

"And the failure of my marriage coupled with the failure of the business, it was a lot for me to take all at once."

"The business isn't a failure," Oliver said. "Or, it doesn't have to be. I read most of Mrs. Chestnut's plan. I think it could work. At the very least it's worth a try."

"That's off the table," Trip said. "I kissed Tom's wife. He's never going to agree to a partnership now."

"Like you said," Oliver reminded him, "the kiss meant nothing." Though, was that even possible? Didn't kisses always mean something to someone? They didn't have to mean "true love" or even "I like you," but they might mean "I'm lonely or sad or happy" or "I just needed to feel something tonight."

"Tell that to Tom Chestnut."

"Are we still moving back to Florida?" Oliver asked.

"I don't see what other choice we have."

"We could stay here, try to make the business work. You don't give up on things, Dad."

"I think this time I have to." Trip stood and patted Oliver on the hand. "I know your sister makes fun of you for it, but maybe you have the right idea," he said. "Keep your head down, and focus on the work. Avoid drama. I envy you, Oliver. You're much stronger than I am."

Trip left the room, closing the door behind him. Oliver swiveled around to face the computer. Out of habit, he opened the Wizard War window. His dad envied him. His dad envied a guy who'd been holed up in his room all day playing video games. He envied a person who hadn't showered in twenty-four hours because he was too busy forcing himself into a state of numbness.

Yeah, that was enviable.

The truth was maybe Oliver had had it all figured out, maybe his system had worked perfectly, but only before he started chatting with proud_hoser and learned what he was missing. Once he'd let her into his life, his plan to remain emotionally anesthetized was ruined. He couldn't go back. He'd spent a whole day trying to go back, and it wasn't working. He was no longer an unfeeling robot. The Tin Man had grown a heart.

Oliver read Elena's texts again, and wrote, "Let's talk."

He deleted it. He couldn't just text her. That was the cheap and easy way out. He blew her off last night without explanation. And even after he did that, she was the one who reached out to him. She'd already texted him twice and he'd ignored her. A message wouldn't be enough. It wouldn't prove to her how much she meant to him or how desperately he wanted this to work or that if she let him kiss her, it would not be meaningless for him. Kissing Elena would be Stash Grab plus Wizard World times a million. Kissing her would be everything.

He called Harper, and she answered after the first ring. "You asshole."

"I know," Oliver said. "But I need your help. I'm going to make things right. Or at least less wrong."

Chapter Fifteen

When Elena arrived at Santabucks the next morning just before six, Craig and Dinesh were the only ones there, aside from Jamison, the barista. The two guys sat at a table together in the back corner of the café, shoulders hunched over their large mugs of steaming black coffee.

Elena nodded to them. "You ready for this?"

Dinesh squinted against the glare of the rising sun. Two gray bags had settled beneath his eyes. "Four more hours." With shaking hands, he lifted his cup to his mouth and sipped, like the coffee was his last remaining tether to the living world.

"D and I were up late last night, planning our attack," Craig explained. "The leader board went dark at midnight, so we have no way of knowing who's winning at this point. There's a long road ahead, and we're going to win those tickets."

"Good luck," Elena said.

"You don't mean that," said Craig.

"No, I don't." She wandered over to the counter, ordered her own black coffee, and checked the time on her phone. It was now five minutes until six. The final four hours of Stash Grab were due to start at six on the dot, and Harper was late. Elena was about to text her best friend that she wasn't going to wait around for her, especially not when Harper was the one who had insisted Elena show up at Santabucks at five-fifty, when the door to Santabucks opened, and Harper hobbled in.

Waving, she yelled toward an idling pickup truck near the curb. "Thanks for the ride, Sam!" Harper struggled, juggling the door, her crutch, and a cone-shaped package. Elena hopped up and gave Harper a hand with the cone.

"What's this?" Elena asked, examining the parcel.

Harper hobbled to Elena's table and motioned to Jamison that she'd like her regular order, thanks. "That's for you," said Harper, pointing to the package. "Open it." Harper, smirking, folded her arms across her chest while Elena, brow furrowed, unwrapped the cone.

Elena's heart stopped when she saw what was inside. A yellow rose. One perfect yellow rose. She dropped it onto the table like it had burned her. "What's this about?"

"I think you know," said Harper, who accepted her to-go vanilla latte from Jamison.

"I don't want it," Elena said.

"Fine." Harper shrugged. "No skin off my back. I only promised I'd give it to you."

The loud scraping of chairs against linoleum cut through the quiet café. Dinesh and Craig shot up, shoved on their coats, and bolted from the store without a word of goodbye to anyone. Elena checked her phone. It was six o'clock. The final stretch of Stash Grab had begun. She glanced at her friend's busted foot. Harper was only going to slow her down. Elena would never win the plane tickets if she had to help Harper limp around town.

Harper caught Elena staring and said, "I know what you're thinking, and I don't blame you. I'm a liability. Leave me here. Save yourself."

"I'm not going to abandon you."

"Yes, you are," Harper said. "I'm finally totally over Regina, and I need to work on my lady-flirting skills." She winked at Jamison, the cute barista with the short, black hair. "It's why I asked you to meet me at Santabucks anyway."

"Thanks." Elena saluted her friend, grabbed her coffee, and started for the door.

Harper stopped her. "Your rose," she said.

"You keep it." Elena took one last glance at the perfect yellow bloom. "I don't want it."

Main Street teemed with Stash Grabbers, more than Elena had seen in a while. The final push for Stashes had motivated everyone to start grabbing again, even those near the bottom of the list. Elena studied her screen. There was a Stash right across the street in Frosty's Dye and Trim. Elena trudged into the barbershop, shaking off her boots on the way in. Don Patrick, AKA Frosty, waved to her as he swept up some hair clippings.

"You're open early," said Elena.

"Stash Grab," he said, holding up a finger. "I have something for you. Wait a minute."

Elena rolled her eyes as she caught the easy twenty-five point Stash in the shop. She didn't have time for this. Don probably had a coupon or something for her to give her dad to entice him to come back for a haircut.

When he returned, Don was holding another yellow rose, just as perfect as the last one. Had Oliver seriously placed a rose in every single North Pole store? Did he really think this would be enough to win her trust? He had stood her up and then ignored every single one of her texts. He had some nerve. "This is for you," Don said.

She accepted it, then dumped it in the garbage can right outside the store.

Elena ducked into Santa's Suit Dry Cleaners next door. There she caught a one-hundred-point Stash and grabbed a caramel bull's eye from the candy dish. Mrs. Ra, the owner, produced yet another yellow rose from under her cash register.

"That Oliver's a nice boy," Mrs. Ra said.

"I don't know about that." Elena stared at the bloom lying on the countertop.

"He likes you a lot." Mrs. Ra grinned. "He was running all over town with these roses." She nudged the flower toward Elena, who made a move to grab it.

No. So he put a few flowers in a few stores. Anyone could do that. It didn't prove that he wouldn't bail on her again when things got tough.

"You keep the rose," she said.

Feeling a sense of dread, Elena marched into the flower shop. But there were no yellow roses to be found there. Elena relaxed.

"I told the Prince boy I wouldn't sell him any flowers," said Bobbi Moore, with a pinched face.

"Good for you." Elena clicked on a Stash and answered the seventy-five-point question.

"His game has been nothing but a nuisance."

"That's right, it has." Elena shoved her phone into her pocket. She turned toward Bobbi, who was now struggling to hold a massive bouquet of yellow roses that had apparently materialized out of thin air. Elena backed toward the door, the oppressive scent of roses clogging her nostrils. What was Oliver trying to do to her? Wear her down? She backed toward the door. A couple of flowers were not going to sway her. She was tougher than that.

Bobbi stepped around the counter. "He showed up at my house last night and fixed my broken fence. Then he offered to create a new website for my business, not that I need one.

Computers are pure evil."

Elena really did not have time for a lecture on the great electronic menace. She had Stashes to catch. "Thank you, Bobbi!" Her hand searched for the door handle.

"Wait," Bobbi said.

Against her better judgment, Elena did.

"Oliver said he knew how much I hated the game and how loath I'd be to help. He told me he never would've come to me if it weren't an emergency." Bobbi held the flowers out to Elena. "Take the flowers, hon. He wrote you a note."

Sighing, Elena wrapped her arms around the unwieldy bouquet. Bobbi held the door open as Elena left the shop. On the sidewalk, for one quick second, Elena considered dumping both the flowers and the card in the trash, but she caught herself. It couldn't hurt to read what he'd written. It wasn't like his words would change anything.

She set the flowers on the ground and opened the card. The message said, "Dear Elena, I can't make up for what I did. I should've called. I should've texted. I definitely shouldn't have shut you out. I've spent the past two days regretting standing you up. I thought I could go back to retreating into my games and hiding behind the computer, but I can't. I miss you. You've ruined me." There was a smiley face after that. "I understand if you can't forgive me, but I hope the flowers, at least, bring you some joy. Kick all the ass at Stash Grab today. Love, Oliver."

Elena's eyes scanned the crowds rushing up and down Main Street. When she realized she was hunting for a thatch of auburn hair, she shook some sense into her brain. This changed nothing. She picked up the flowers and hurled them and the note into the garbage can next to Bobbi's flower shop. Elena checked her phone. There was a Stash in the bakery.

She caught that one and accepted another rose from Dottie, which she tossed in the garbage on the way out.

Then Mr. Wong in The Chinese Restaurant gave her a flower. So did Maurice in the video store, and Reverend Michaels in the church. Each rose went into a trashcan on Main Street.

Needing to clear her head, she ran all the way to the edge of town and into Ludlum's Grocery Store. She caught a quick Stash in the feminine hygiene aisle, and rolled her eyes when Gretchen Ludlum, whose dad was the grocer, presented her with another rose.

"Keep it, Gretchen."

Elena had gone to the back of the store to grab a bottle of water, when a voice startled her.

"Fancy meeting you here."

She turned toward the voice. There was her dad, holding one of the refrigerator doors open.

"Hi, Dad."

He pulled out a carton of milk and held it up. "None left for cereal," he said. "What are you doing out so early?"

Elena winced. "Stash Grab. Last day."

Her dad shook his head.

"So…how are you and Mom doing?" She hadn't seen either of them since the store yesterday. They were sleeping when she got home last night, and were still in bed when she left this morning.

Her dad grinned, and the dread in Elena's stomach melted. "We're okay. We've decided that both of us, for our health, should stay as far away from Trip Prince as possible. I think I'm finally at peace about the whole situation."

Elena glanced up as the door to the grocery store opened and in walked Oliver Prince and his father. "Latch on tight to that peaceful feeling," Elena said through gritted teeth.

Her dad spun toward the door, and, when he spotted Trip, gripped the milk carton so tight Elena feared he'd burst it all over the refrigerated section of the grocery store. Elena patted her dad's hand. "Breathe in. Breathe out."

Trip marched toward them, on a mission, and Oliver followed behind, his hair flopping against his face. He glanced up when he reached Elena, and his eyes went right to her hands, which were empty. "You're not catching Stashes today?"

"Oh, I am," she said, folding her arms. She avoided his gaze, because she knew his eyes would make rejecting him almost impossible.

He frowned. "Has anyone given you…?"

"Roses?" she asked. "They sure have. I don't want them, thanks."

"I was here first, Trip," said Elena's dad as he boxed out Trip Prince, preventing him from getting to the freezers. Glad for the distraction, Elena turned her back on Oliver.

"I'm just picking up some ice for the Stash Grab event." Trip elbowed Tom Chestnut out of the way and flung open the freezer door.

Clearly, this store wasn't big enough for the both of them. "Dad, let him get the ice," Elena said.

"That stupid game." Tom rubbed the spot on his ribcage where Trip had just jammed his elbow. "Thank God it's almost over. Nothing but a pain in the ass."

"Says who?" Trip frowned.

"Lots of people," Tom said. "Bobbi Moore."

Trip laughed. "Bobbi Moore! You can't go by Bobbi Moore! Everything bugs her."

"Did you stop by Bobbi Moore's store this morning?" Oliver whispered from behind Elena.

"Yes." She waved him off and focused hard on their fathers. Oliver seriously did think a few flowers and one little note would be enough.

"Bobbi has some very valid complaints about the game." Tom folded his arms.

"I'm sure she does," Trip said. "Bobbi's full of complaints."

Tom chuckled, his eyes softening, but he stopped himself quickly. Elena couldn't help smiling, but she forced herself not to turn toward Oliver, even though she wondered if he was wearing a similar grin.

Trip, his eyes on Tom, said, "Hey, remember when we'd play baseball in your backyard and our balls would land in her shrubs?"

"Only once in a while," added Tom with a little eye-roll. "We were pretty good at keeping our stuff on Chestnut property."

"That we were."

Now Elena did turn around. Oliver's mouth had dropped open, and she knew what he was thinking. Their dads were talking in normal, almost friendly tones. She and Oliver were watching a miracle happen. Elena held her index finger to her lips. *Don't ruin it.*

"Ha," Trip said. "But whenever we'd hit one into her yard, Bobbi would come over and shriek at us."

"I don't want your balls near me!" they yelled in unison.

Everyone in the store spun toward the back.

Tom straightened his shoulders and cleared his throat. "It was always your fault," he said. "You were the one who'd hit into her yard."

Trip narrowed his eyes. "You're just jealous that I could hit farther than you."

"Bullshit," said Tom.

"Not bullshit." Trip stepped toward Tom.

"I'd miss the ball on purpose to make you feel better, because you sucked at baseball." Elena's dad scrunched up his face and pretended to cry. "Poor Trip, always sad when someone beat him at something." He glared. "You could never handle losing, as a kid or as an adult."

Trip's neck was bright red, and Elena shot Oliver a

warning look.

"Come on, you two," Oliver said. "You used to be friends."

"Ha, friends," Trip said. "You've always been jealous of me, Tom. You were jealous of me and Emily. Now you're jealous my store is doing better than yours—"

"Your store that's about to close?" said Tom.

"By choice. My choice. Your store's the one that's about to go under," Trip said.

He and Tom were now nose to nose. Oliver took charge. He slid himself between his dad and Elena's. Then he nudged Trip's chest and guided his dad toward the front of the store. "We'll get the ice somewhere else."

As he and his dad reached the door, Oliver glanced back at Elena, and their eyes met. He put his hand to his heart and mouthed, "I'm sorry."

Elena shook her head, and then stared at the door after it had shut behind him.

"Good riddance." Her dad raised his jug of milk in salute. "This town will be better off without those Princes."

"Yeah," she said.

Empty handed, Elena left the store and headed back toward town. She checked her phone. There was a half hour left of Stash Grab. She ducked into the gun store, where Katie Murphy was working. Katie, of course, handed Elena one perfect yellow rose, and her heart sank.

"You're so lucky," said Katie.

Elena wrinkled her nose. "Why?"

"Oliver really likes you. He came in here all passionate and disheveled like, 'I have to get Elena to forgive me.'" She touched the back of her hand to her forehead like she was about to swoon. "The only romance I've had lately was kissing Kevin Snow under Harper's dining room table."

Elena rolled her eyes. "I've been there." She examined the rose. Oliver had run all over town last night, leaving roses for her in every store. But the flowers weren't just from Oliver Prince, the guy she'd been trained to see as the scum of the earth. They were from Stashiuk4Prez, the guy she'd spent the past few weeks opening up to. They were from Oliver, whom she'd run around town with catching Stashes. They were from the person who stepped in and kept their fathers from killing each other.

She could forget all the good and focus on the bad. She could toss this rose in the garbage with the rest. She could keep holding this grudge, just like her dad and Oliver's dad had for twenty years.

Elena glanced outside. The garbage truck was making its way down Main Street. One of the trash collectors hopped off the truck and emptied the can right outside the yoga studio. She caught sight of a yellow rose toppling into the back of the truck and being devoured by the massive, steel teeth. Her heart ached.

Yes, they were only flowers, but they were hers. They represented what she and Oliver meant to each other, and Elena had just witnessed the metaphor for their romance being chopped up into tiny pieces. She would not let another flower wind up in that truck.

She dashed out onto the street, waving the flower Katie had given her, and shouted, "Wait!"

· · ·

Oliver steered his dad down Main Street, through the Stash Grab crowds and toward Prince's.

"We didn't get the ice," his dad said, glancing back toward the grocery store.

"I'll go back out." Oliver pushed his dad through the door and into the sporting goods shop. Trip quickly busied himself behind the counter, and Oliver motioned for Regina, who had been setting up chairs in the middle of the floor, to convene with him in the office.

Oliver checked on his dad one more time—he was counting money in the till—and shut the door behind Regina. "We just ran into Mr. Chestnut in the grocery store." *And Elena*, thought Oliver, remembering the distraught look on her face as he pushed his dad through the door. But he'd worry about her later. First he had to work on their parents. "There was…a moment," Oliver said.

"A moment?" Regina plopped down onto the desk chair.

"Yeah." Oliver paced the length of the office. "A moment where they didn't hate each other."

"Really?"

"They were talking about Bobbi Moore and how she hated them when they were kids. I saw it. They bonded." Oliver pointed to the closed door. "Dad got wistful."

Regina shrugged. "And?"

"And, I think we can use that to our advantage. I think it proves there's hope for a peaceful accord between Dad and the Chestnuts." He snapped his fingers, then bent down and extracted the infamous photo album from the bottom drawer. He handed it to Regina. "I have a plan…I think." He glanced at the clock. It was nine now. One hour until the Stash Grab event. He laughed. Plenty of time. "Here's what I need you to do. I need you to scan all these pictures and make a PowerPoint for the Stash Grab event. We're going to have a projector set up anyway for the retrospective video."

Regina scoffed. "Okay, weird."

Oliver shook his head. "You want to stay in North Pole?" She nodded.

"Then start PowerPointing. Microsoft Office Suite is our last, best hope."

Oliver left her alone at the laptop with her assignment. He shut the door and leaned against it. Now for phase two.

"Dad." Oliver pulled on his hat and mittens. "I'm gonna go get that ice."

"Great." Trip was still focused on the money.

Oliver booked it out of the store and, dodging the crowds of people with their heads down on their phones, ran all the way to Elena's house without stopping. He stood on the top step of the Chestnuts' stoop, took off his hat, and smoothed down his hair. Then he rang the bell.

Mrs. Chestnut, in pajama pants and a robe, answered the door. "Yes?"

"Hi, Mrs. Chestnut. I'm Oliver Prince."

"I know," she said, pulling her robe tighter.

"Can I talk to you for a minute? And Mr. Chestnut, too?"

She glanced behind her. Oliver couldn't tell if she was looking for a way out of this or making sure her husband hadn't seen his rival's son standing on their doorstep.

"Please," Oliver said. "It's about my dad. It's important."

Frowning, Mrs. Chestnut stepped aside and let him in. "Take a seat," she said, pointing to the living room couch.

Oliver removed his boots and perched on the edge of the couch cushion, hands folded in his lap. He glanced around the room. There were pictures of Elena all over—in a track and field uniform, dressed up for a dance, making goofy faces with Harper. Oliver's toes tapped on the floor. *This is for her*, he thought. *This is for us*.

When Mrs. Chestnut returned with her husband, Oliver stood and held out his hand. "Mr. Chestnut, hi."

Ignoring Oliver's outstretched arm, Mr. Chestnut motioned for Oliver to sit, then he sat on one of the arm chairs near the fireplace. Mrs. Chestnut poured coffee for everyone before taking a spot on the other end of the couch from Oliver.

No one spoke, and Oliver realized that it was up to him to get the conversation started. "Okay," he said, clearing his throat. "My dad sent me here." Oliver prayed his lying skills were up to snuff. This was just a video game, essentially. He needed to complete each level before moving onto the next. No big deal. "The whole way home after we ran into you at the grocery store, he kept talking about your conversation and how sad he was that it had turned sour. He wanted me to come here and invite you—in person—to attend the Stash Grab event, which starts in an hour. He wants to make amends."

Tom Chestnut furrowed his brow. "Why did he send you? If it meant so much to him, why didn't he come himself?"

This was a test. It was only a test. "Because he's Trip. You know Trip, his showmanship. I think he wants to make a big display out of apologizing to you."

Mr. Chestnut nodded, and a weight lifted from Oliver's chest. But then he said, "No, I don't think so."

"Tom, please," his wife said.

"We're leaving anyway, Emily. What's the point? I don't want anything to do with Trip, and I know he wants nothing to do with me."

"Please, Mr. Chestnut—" Oliver said. He had to come, he just had to.

Mr. Chestnut stood, looming over his wife and Oliver. "I'm sorry. No. I have no interest in making peace with Trip Prince." He marched out of the room, and Mrs. Chestnut and Oliver stared after him.

A few moments later, Mrs. Chestnut ushered Oliver to the door. As she handed him his hat, she whispered, "I'll get him there."

Oliver's eyes met hers. They were brown and determined, just like Elena's. He nodded. "Thank you."

Next Oliver ran back to the grocery store to pick up some ice for real. Then he, panting, jogged back to Prince's.

"What took you so long?" asked Trip. "People are going to be here in fifteen minutes, and your sister has locked herself in the office."

"She has Stash Grab business to take care of," said Oliver, pouring the ice into a cooler. "Hey, Dad," he said. "I ran into Tom Chestnut on Main Street."

His dad grumbled.

"He felt bad about how your conversation in the grocery store ended. He told me he wanted to stop by the event today, to publicly apologize for hurting you."

"Hmph," said Trip. "Doesn't sound like him."

"I know," said Oliver. "But I think you really got through to him today."

Trip rolled his eyes and started rearranging the chairs Regina had only just set up in the middle of Prince's.

Oliver made sure everything was ready at the refreshments table, which reminded him of the time he had helped Elena set up the food at her Stash Grab Dash event. He smacked himself on the forehead. The cheeseless pizza. She had seen him grab a slice. He bet that was when she knew he and Stashiuk4Prez were one in the same. If today ended better than that night did, Oliver's plan would be a success.

At ten o'clock sharp, Oliver knocked on the office door. "Time for the party," he told Regina.

He threw open the front entrance, and scores of North Pole residents flooded in. Oliver greeted Craig and Dinesh, who were first in line. He saw Danny, Star, Kevin, Brian, and Marley, plus Dolores Page and Frank from the hardware store, Sam and Maurice from the video store, Mr. Patrick, Mrs. Ra, Mr. Wong, Bobbi Moore, and Sheriff Parsons. Bringing up the rear, Harper tottered in on the arm of Jamison, the Santabucks barista.

Oliver peered past her, looking for stragglers.

Harper patted his shoulder. "I haven't seen her."

Oliver took his spot on the makeshift stage, between his dad and Stan Stashiuk. Oliver's dad was keeping an eye on the front door as well.

As the mayor stepped up to the podium, the office door flew open and Regina, carrying the laptop, ran onto the stage and plugged the machine into the projector that had been set up for the Stash Grab retrospective video. She flopped onto the seat next to Stash. "Just in time," she said.

Mayor Sandoval stepped to the microphone. "Welcome, everyone, to the first ever Stash Grab results extravaganza! Thank you all for participating in this game. I've never seen so much cooperation and excitement in this town—at least not during the months of January and February. The spirit of North Pole extends far beyond December. The Prince twins have put together a video of some of our favorite Stash Grab memories." He stepped aside as Regina pressed play.

On the screen and accompanied by the song "One Shining Moment," like at the end of the NCAA basketball tournament, photos danced by in quick succession—Craig and Dinesh wrestling some high school soccer players over a Stash, Jimmy Shaw showing off his frostbitten fingers, Dolores Page jamming her tongue down Frank the hardware store owner's throat, and more. Oliver kept an eye on the front door, but the Chestnuts never came in. When the last picture had been star-wiped away, Regina pressed stop.

The mayor resumed his place in front of the microphone. "Now is the time we've all been waiting for."

Stan Stashiuk stood just off to the mayor's left, holding a comically large facsimile of an airline ticket.

"We're here to announce the winner of the first ever North Pole Stash Grab competition. First prize, of course, gets the airline tickets provided by Bronze Air."

"Go for the Bronze," muttered Stash.

"First prize also gets two hundred dollars to spend at Prince's, as well as a signed Stan Stashiuk hockey sweater."

Regina handed the mayor an envelope, and then sat back

down. She leaned across the empty chair between herself and Oliver. "How's your plan going?"

He shook his head furiously, willing the door to open.

Mayor Sandoval opened the envelope and said, "Third prize, winning fifty dollars to Prince's, goes to…drumroll, please."

The crowd began a makeshift drumroll.

"Third prize goes to…Dolores Page!"

Dolores Page strutted to the front of the store, arms raised in victory.

As he handed her the prize envelope, the mayor asked, "What will you buy with the money?"

"I might buy something my grandchildren will enjoy when they visit me here."

The crowd released a collective, "Aww!"

"Or maybe I'll put it toward a new surfboard for when I go see my son in California."

"I hope you have good insurance," the mayor said as Dolores headed back to her seat next to Frank. "The second place finisher gets a one hundred dollar gift card to Prince's. The winner is…Dinesh Chauhan!"

Dinesh high-fived Craig before climbing the dais and claiming his prize.

"Where's Tom?" Trip whispered to Oliver.

"I don't know," he hissed, his heart in his throat. This wasn't going to work. He'd miscalculated. He'd completed every single task, but he still failed the mission.

"And the big winner is…" The mayor leaned in close to the mic, as Danny rose from his seat. "Our own Craig Cooper!"

Danny flopped back into his seat and crossed his arms, frowning. Star patted his shoulder.

Craig pumped his fists and ran a lap before finally making his way to the stage. The mayor handed him his envelope full of prizes, and Craig launched into his victory speech.

"I want to thank you all for this great honor," said Craig. "I promise to respect the title and not besmirch the crown."

"There's no crown," the mayor whispered.

Craig kept going. "I love North Pole more than anything. This town represents all that is good and pure in the world. It is truly the greatest place on the planet. Also, if any of you beautiful ladies are free tonight, Dinesh and I are looking—"

The mayor tried to box Craig out of the way as the door to Prince's opened. Everyone swung around to see who had entered. There, framed in the doorway, were the silhouettes of two people—Mr. and Mrs. Chestnut.

Oliver peered past them, searching for Elena, but she wasn't with her parents. They had come alone. "Press play," Oliver whispered to his sister.

Regina leaned over and began her PowerPoint presentation. The first photos up on screen were of the original Prince and Chestnut's, which had been opened fifty years ago by Tom and Trip's fathers.

The audience stared at the picture for a moment, but quickly started murmuring when there was no sound to accompany the slideshow.

"Say something," Regina hissed.

Oliver, who didn't like to get involved, and who usually tried to blend in with the walls at school, stood and took the microphone from the mayor. "Hi," he said. "My sister and I put together this little presentation to honor the two sporting goods stores that have served this town for the past fifty years." Oohs and awws sounded from the audience as the pictures rolled by, photos of his dad and Tom Chestnut as young boys. "I don't know if everybody knows this, but both stores will be shuttering their doors soon. We Princes are moving back to Florida and the Chestnuts are going to Wisconsin."

The mumbling in the audience went from amused to

concerned.

"What?" yelled Frank from the hardware store. "You can't do that."

"Where will I buy my Sex Wax?" asked Dolores Page. "What?" she said, glancing around at shocked faces. "For my *surfboard*."

Oliver kept talking. "I've only been here for a few months, but already North Pole feels like home. I'm going to miss it."

"Boo!" sang a chorus from the audience.

Trip stood behind Oliver and leaned into the microphone. "We can't survive here. Neither store is doing well."

"We need a fresh start," shouted Tom Chestnut from the back of the store.

Oliver glanced back at the PowerPoint presentation happening behind him. It was the photo of his dad hugging Mrs. Chestnut with Mr. Chestnut smiling in the background.

The mayor noticed it, too, and stepped up to the mic. "Tom and Trip, you guys always said you'd bring the stores back together when you were in charge."

"Circumstances have changed." Tom folded his arms.

"He stole my fiancée," Trip said.

"He kissed my wife," Tom said.

"Bah, bah, bah." Mags from the diner stood up, though she was so tiny, her head barely cleared the rest of the crowd.

"Come on up here, Mags," said the mayor.

Oliver stepped aside as Mags took the microphone. "You two were thick as thieves growing up. I remember. We all do." She gestured to the picture behind her of Trip and Tom tossing their caps after their high school graduation. "And neither of you has been the same since you stopped being friends." She pointed to Tom near the door. "You have thrown yourself into the store. You're good with ideas, less good with business. You've been searching for a buddy this whole time, at the barbershop or playing ball in the park, but no one could hold a candle to Trip. And you," she spun around and glared at Trip, "you're the money man, but you're stuck in your own ways. Plus, you've been searching so hard for a friend since you've been back, you turned to Tom's wife, of all people. Can't you two guys see you're made for each other?"

"No," Trip and Tom shouted at the same time as Mags wandered back to the audience.

Leaning on Jamison, Harper stood. "It's time for the feud to end! Because of this stupid feud, Oliver and Elena spent most of the year hating each other instead of realizing they belonged together."

Oliver blushed, and the door to Prince's opened. Elena stepped in. Her hair was a mess, but she was carrying a mangled bouquet of yellow roses.

He took the mic from his dad. "Harper's right," he said. "I had been taught my entire life to hate the Chestnuts, that they're not to be trusted. But you know what's not to be trusted? The feud itself. The feud is toxic. The feud is the reason both stores are closing. The feud is the reason you two"—he pointed to his dad and Tom—"have to keep pretending you don't want to let bygones be bygones. The feud is what has kept me from doing this." He handed the microphone to the mayor and marched down the stairs, past the rows and rows of prying eyes. He stood in front of Elena, who had a smudge of dirt on her face and her damp hair clung to her cheeks.

"I got all the flowers. Or, well, most of them. I saved them from the garbage truck," she said, nodding toward the massive bouquet she was cradling in both arms. "Katie at the gun store gave me a rose and I was about to chuck that one into the garbage, too, with the rest, but I couldn't. I didn't want to. I wanted the flowers. I want you."

Grinning, Oliver cupped her face in his hands, leaned down, and kissed her in front of his dad, her parents, and the entire population of North Pole, Minnesota.

Chapter Sixteen

All that mattered in the entire universe were Oliver's hands on Elena's face, his nose against her cheek, and his soft lips on hers. It wasn't just the sensation of him touching her, but the melding of their breaths, his scent of clove and citrus, and the fact that, even through her parka, Elena could feel his heart beating, like it was trying its damnedest to reach hers.

When he pulled away, Elena let out a tiny, accidental sob. She wasn't ready for it to be over. She'd never be ready. But as the space between them grew, Elena remembered she and Oliver were not alone. Far from it. The entire town was there with them, having shifted in their seats to watch the show. And they were clapping, applauding her and Oliver, like this was a Broadway show they'd paid top dollar for.

Sam Anderson let out a piercing whistle, and the mayor tap-tap-tapped on the microphone. "We're all very happy for you, Oliver and Elena, but that hasn't solved anything, now has it?"

Elena was sure it solved plenty, and she reached for Oliver's hand. He laced his fingers between hers and squeezed.

"A-hem," came a voice from nearby. The entire town swung its collective consciousness to the right of the front door. Elena's mom stepped out of the shadows and raised her hand, in which she was holding something shiny. "I brought this with, just in case." She marched to the riser and asked Regina for help with the computer. The PowerPoint disappeared and was replaced by a different document, one entitled "Plan for Prince's and Chestnut's."

"That's the paper I saw," Oliver whispered in Elena's ear. She shivered from his breath. He should always speak to her like that—in a hot whisper, right up against her ear.

Elena's mom grabbed the mic from Mayor Sandoval and said, "I presented this plan to both my husband and Trip a few weeks ago, because I saw the writing on the wall. Our business wasn't doing well, and I could tell that Trip's heart wasn't in his store. Back in college, like you said, Mayor"—she nodded to Mayor Sandoval—"Trip and Tom used to talk about taking over their dads' businesses and recombining them into one store, which I thought was a great idea, but it wouldn't solve one of their major issues." She asked Regina to flip to another screen. "Neither store has enough space. There are too many sports with too much equipment taking up too much room. We're not able to stock everything we need."

"It's true," said Craig. "Neither store carries my preferred brand of athletic cup."

"He's not kidding," Elena whispered to Oliver. "I have to special order them at least twice a year."

"If this plan goes through," Oliver whispered, "we'll stock the cups at Prince's so you never have to think about protecting Craig's junk again."

"How does he go through that many cups? What is he doing with them?"

"I think it's better if we don't ask questions," said Oliver.

"Thank you, Craig," said Elena's mom. "So, what I've

looked into, and not to get too bogged down in specifics, but what if we merged the stores and split the sports? Chestnut's could handle winter and fall, because, come on, 'Chestnut's' screams winter, and Prince's could do spring and summer."

"Paying two rents on essentially one store?" asked Frank.

"If we wanted to keep it one store, we'd have to rent a bigger space, and our current rates are rent-controlled. It makes more sense this way. Plus, we can focus more staff to either store, depending on the time of year."

The mayor grabbed the microphone back. "But the real question here is, would we, the people of North Pole, patronize both stores—one for winter, and one for summer? Would we help them stay afloat?"

"Yes!" the crowd cheered.

"It's up to Trip and Tom," said Elena's mom.

The two of them frowned at each other.

Elena's mom spoke again. "I've known you two for years. The mayor's right. Tom loves me, but he misses you, Trip. He needs you. You need each other. Let's stay here and fight for your families' legacies. If it doesn't work, it doesn't work, but if it does—"

Tom and Trip met each other in the middle and shook hands.

. . .

"You guys make me sick," complained Sam. "All of you."

"Maybe find yourself a girlfriend and you won't feel so vomit-y." Harper grinned at Jamison, who was sitting on the couch next to her, one arm draped across Harper's shoulders.

The crowd had gathered in the Andersons' basement for a trilogy of Sam-approved movies. Danny and Star were lying on the floor together. Regina and Stan Stashiuk had commandeered Mr. Anderson's favorite recliner. And Oliver and Elena had attached themselves at the hip on the other end of the couch from Harper and Jamison.

Oliver smiled down at Elena. It had been a heady day—seeing the end of Stash Grab, watching their fathers shake hands in front of the entire town, and then having to sit down for lunch to hash things out as a combined Chestnut-Prince unit. But the thing that saved him was the fact that Elena was by his side the entire time. He squeezed her knee and she rested her head on his shoulder.

"Where am I supposed to sit?" Sam put his hands on his hips. Despite it being twenty degrees outside, he was still wearing his mesh basketball shorts. Feuds end, enemies fall in love, but some things never change.

"You can cuddle with us, Sam," Regina teased as she coiled Stash's curls around her fingers.

Sam shook his head and plopped onto the couch between Jamison and Elena, who scooted closer to Oliver. He pulled her in tight and kissed her hair, breathing her in.

The movie was some subtitled Italian horror flick Sam had chosen, and there was no way Oliver was going to be able to pay attention to that, not with everything that had happened today, and not with Elena next to him, smelling like cinnamon gum and grapefruit shampoo.

About twenty minutes in, he whispered, "This movie is terrible, right?"

"The worst," she said.

"I can't hear what they're saying," Sam warned, gesturing toward the television.

"You don't have to hear," Harper said. "The movie is subtitled."

Elena grabbed Oliver's hand and led him up to the kitchen, where she made them a plate of leftover cookies from the Stash Grab event. Oliver stood at the back window, looking out on the Andersons' snow-covered backyard.

Elena stood next to him, thoughtfully chewing a snickerdoodle. "I feel like we've done this before."

"The night of Harper's birthday party," he said. "When everyone was out there hunting Stashes." He nodded toward the pier.

"And I was stuck standing here with you. That Stash could've put me over the edge for those plane tickets." She nudged him in the side. "Curses!"

"What about spring break?" he asked.

"You know," said Elena, "I think I made enough tutoring your ass that I'll be able to go. You can teach me how to wrestle alligators. It's only fair. I taught you how to skate." She gazed up at him and her big brown eyes crinkled with laughter.

"That's debatable."

Elena nodded toward the backyard, where the Andersons had made a huge ice rink for Harper's little sister Maddie to practice on. "Want another lesson?"

They threw on their boots and coats and trudged through the drifts out to the backyard. Elena, who was much better in the snow than Oliver was, helped him navigate the high piles on the way to the rink.

She turned toward the next-door neighbor's house, a big abandoned log cabin. "Wow, it's for sale," she said. "No one's lived there for as long as Harper's been in her house."

"That's cool," Oliver said. "I hope whoever moves in isn't part of a nasty, decades-long feud with anyone else in North Pole."

"Too true."

She led him over one final hill and onto the ice, where she clutched his mittened hands and dragged him to the middle of the rink.

"So," she said.

"So." He smiled, forgetting momentarily that his face was

about to freeze off. "Are we gonna skate?"

"We're gonna skate," she said.

"Because I'm nearly a block of ice at this point."

She winced. "We can go back in, if you want."

He shook his head. "Frostbite can't hurt me. I'm with Elena Chestnut."

"Pretty sure it can still hurt you."

He pulled off his mitten and caressed her cheek. She leaned into his hand. "Remind me why we hated each other?"

"I never hated you," she said.

"Oh, you sure did."

"Eh, you're right. I did." Her eyes met his, and she pulled him in close. Oliver wrapped his arms around her and bent to kiss her. How he could've ever believed video games were a good substitute for this was beyond him. This was real. This was flesh and breath and cold winds and puffy, down parkas. He ran a hand down Elena's silky dark hair, and a snowball smacked him right in the temple. Cold water dripped down his cheek and onto his coat.

Oliver and Elena pulled apart and found Danny, Star, Sam, Regina, and Stan Stashiuk standing on the snowdrifts, ready to pelt them with snowballs. Jamison and Harper watched from the deck. Oliver pulled on his glove as Elena dashed toward their tormentors, firing snowball after snowball. "Avenge me, my Florida boy!" she called.

"I've got your back." He reached down, formed his own perfect snowball, and charged after her, ready to fight.

Epilogue

"The soccer display should go over here," said Trip Prince.

"You sure?" asked Tom Chestnut, stroking his chin. "I think it's better over on this side where there's a little more room. People want to test out the balls—"

"In my *store*? They're going to be kicking balls around my *store*?" Trip asked.

"Around *our* store," said Tom. "And, yes, sometimes people want to test out the merchandise. We should put up a goal—"

The two men lumbered, still arguing, toward the back, and Elena gave her mom a smile. The four of them, and Harper, were working hard setting up the new stores—Prince's Spring and Summer Sports and Chestnut's Winter Sports Emporium. Since the last day of Stash Grab three weeks ago, both families had been working together almost nonstop to figure out their vision for the stores.

Elena, who was tidying up behind the counter, glanced outside. Across the street at Chestnut's, a man was hanging the store's new sign. He kept wiping his face as the icicles on the roof melted into his eyes. The sun was shining today and the temperature had crept above freezing for the first time in recent memory. North Pole residents ambled down the street toward church, wearing lighter coats over their Sunday clothes. The Joyce family strolled by, sans Christmas sweaters. Spring was truly on its way. Thank goodness, because Elena was done with cold weather. She scratched a bit of peeling skin on her arm.

"Don't pick at it," said Harper, from the stool next to Elena. "God, it's like you've never had a sunburn before."

"Not for a while anyway. How come you're not burned?"

"Because I'm a professional, Elena." The two of them had just gotten back to North Pole yesterday after spending spring break in Florida with Harper's family. The girls spent the entire seven days lounging by the pool, and Elena made sure to run on the beach each morning. "When does your boyfriend get back?"

Elena blushed. "Any minute." She had chosen to work behind the counter mostly because it meant she could keep a close eye on the front door. While the Prince twins had originally planned to hang out with the Andersons and Elena on Captiva Island for break, they decided instead to visit their mom in Florida, since they both wanted to live in North Pole with their dad long-term.

Oliver had texted Elena every night, and she sent him messages all day about what she and Harper were up to—swimming, eating, helping Matthew and Hakeem plan their wedding, which would be in North Pole this summer. It had been like she and Oliver were back playing Stash Grab, communicating only through texts. It was comforting, but Elena missed the real thing.

Eventually, finally, the door to Prince's flew open and in came Oliver and Regina. Elena flew out from behind the counter and grabbed Oliver in a big hug.

"How's your mom?" Elena asked, holding him at arms' length.

Oliver shrugged. "She's doing fine. Good, actually. She, like everybody here"—he nodded toward his father in the back of the store—"seems a bit relieved that the divorce is actually happening and everyone can get on with their lives." He lowered his voice. "We had a nice talk. She regretted all the pressure she put on me, and she's glad I'm making friends." His eyes sparkled. "And she bought me a new laptop."

"Look at you, reaping the rewards of parental guilt." She nudged him in the side.

"You know it," he said.

"Hey, Elena," said her mom, checking her watch. "Can you go open up the store? It's almost eleven."

Elena caught Oliver's eye and nodded toward the exit. He followed her across the street and stood behind her as she unlocked the door to Chestnut's. The inside had been transformed into a winter wonderland. When she flipped on the lights, a mechanical Santa began a chorus of "Ho, ho, ho."

Elena unzipped her coat. "My parents decided, with this being a cold-weather sports store and with their last name being Chestnut, they should really lean into the whole year-round Christmas thing."

Oliver brushed her long, wavy hair behind her ears, then he leaned down and kissed her. She'd been dreaming about this moment for the past week, but reality was so much better. She wrapped her arms around his parka, pulling him in as close as possible, looking forward to the day sometime soon when outerwear might no longer impede their romance.

"We should've taken our coats off first," she said.

"I couldn't wait." He kissed her again, and one more time before she went back to the entrance and flipped the sign on the door to open.

Within minutes, Craig had darkened their doorstep. Elena

took her place behind the counter and Oliver fixed an errant string of Christmas lights on the window, as Craig perused the new store. "I was wondering what deals you might have going on right now. And is there going to be a grand reopening sale?"

Elena snuck a quick peek at Oliver, who was trying hard not to laugh. Elena's whole body warmed with cheer. She no longer needed to deal with Craig on her own. She no longer needed to worry about competing with Prince's for customers. Her family and Oliver's family, they were all in this together. "I'm not sure, Craig," she said. "Possibly?"

Craig held out his phone and showed her the screen. "Because Amazon is offering hockey sticks at half off right now—"

Before Craig could say another word, Oliver said, "Let me show you what we have." Then he whisked Craig off to the back of the store—before Elena could scream or throw something at him or sweep him out of Chestnut's with a broom.

She busied herself behind the counter, tidying up, straightening pictures. Her parents had put up all kinds of Christmas decorations around the store; but through all of the hubbub, they must've forgotten about the photographs on this wall—the shots of the original Prince and Chestnut's and the plaque that read, "We reserve the right to refuse service to any Prince."

Elena plucked the sign off the wall and dropped it in the garbage. She wiped her hands. The feud was over. She knew exactly what she'd put in its place—a picture of all of them together, Oliver and Regina and their dad, Elena and her parents, maybe even Stash and Harper and Danny and Dinesh and Craig and whoever else wanted to be in the photo. Because the merger of Prince and Chestnut's was bigger than Elena and Oliver, and it was bigger than their two families.

These stores belonged to the town, and the town belonged to everyone.

"Elena?" Oliver and Craig stepped out from the hockey aisle. "Did you know there's been a recall on these balaclavas?" Craig held up an open box of winter accessories.

Elena counted to ten in her head, struggling to conceal her annoyance. Then she realized she didn't have to do that. She could look at Oliver's laughing brown eyes instead, and let the calm wash over her. Well, that was much easier.

"Show me, Craig," she said. "And thank you so very much for bringing this to our attention. We live to serve."

Craig frowned. "You're mocking me again."

"Never."

Craig paused a moment, then decided to just go with it. "Well, if that's the case. I notice you're carrying last year's hockey sticks from--"

Elena tuned him out as Oliver joined her behind the counter and wrapped his arm around her waist. She rested her head on his shoulder and watched the window, where a mob of kids was kicking the yoga studio's plastic Rudolph down the street while Mayor Sandoval ran after them, shouting and panting for air. Elena no longer had to pretend she was somewhere else. She was right where she wanted to be.

Acknowledgments

Thank you to all the brilliant folks at Entangled. Kate Brauning, you are an editing genius. I cannot say that enough. Bethany Robison, your encouragement keeps me going. Thank you for doing my research for me and sending me the Christmas town pictures!

Thank you to my agent, Beth Phelan, for making this deal happen. You're always such a wonderful sounding board and an incredible advocate for all your authors.

Thank you, John, for being my first reader on this and all things.

Thanks to my mom, always, for watching my kids whenever I need her to.

And thank you to my dad for that one Thanksgiving weekend where he left the Hallmark Movie Channel on for three days straight. This book never would've existed otherwise.

About the Author

Julie Hammerle is the author of *The Sound of Us* (Entangled Teen, 2016) and the North Pole, Minnesota romance series (Entangled Crush, 2017). She writes about TV and pop culture for the ChicagoNow blog, Hammervision, and lives in Chicago with her family. She enjoys reading, cooking, and watching all the television.

Discover more of Entangled Teen Crush's books...

Pushing the Boundaries
an *Off Limits* novel by Stacey Trombley

Myra goes to Haiti with one goal: take the photograph that will win a scholarship and prove that she has what it takes to be a photographer. Elias might lose his job if he breaks the rule forbidding him from socializing with a client, but this girl Myra insists on going outside the city to capture the perfect picture, and he steps in as her guide in order to keep her safe. The deeper they go into the country, the more they fall for each other. Now they're both taking risks that could cost each other their dreams.

There's Something About Nik
a novel by Sara Hantz

Nik Gustafsson has a secret: He's the son of one of the most important families in Europe. And his posh, too-public life is suffocating him. When he gets the chance to attend boarding school in America, he decides to masquerade as an average student. Then he literally runs into Amber—and she hates him at first sight. It's exhilarating to be hated for who he is, not for his name. But the more he gets to know her, the worse he feels keeping secrets from her.

Weddings, Crushes, and Other Dramas
a *Creative HeArts* novel by Emily McKay

Willa is happy to be the maid of honor in her dad's upcoming wedding. Not as happy about the best man being her soon-to-be stepbrother, the infuriating—and infuriatingly gorgeous—Finn McCain. Every time their paths cross, the attraction simmering between them grows a little harder to ignore. Willa knows Finn only wants what he can't have. But Finn is determined to prove to Willa that happily-ever-after will always be worth the risk.

The Bad Boy Bargain
a novel by Kendra C. Highley

Baseball player Kyle Sawyer has many labels: bad boy, delinquent, ladies' man, fearless outfielder... Only one of them is actually true. But then sweet ballet dancer Faith Gladwell asks him to help wreck her reputation, and everything goes sideways. Faith needs someone to squelch the rumors she's an ice queen. And who better than the school's bad boy to show up her cheating ex? But her plan threatens to expose Sawyer's biggest secret of all...and that's a risk he's not willing to take.

Also by Julie Hammerle...

THE SOUND OF US